Readers love

A Shared Range

"…another enjoyable read filled with two well rounded and likable guys."
—Literary Nymphs

Pump Me Up

"Andrew Grey is a master storyteller. His stories have heart and the characters fairly leap off the pages to completely captivate you."
—Love Romances & More

An Unexpected Vintage

"There's nothing like a story that reminds you to get out and enjoy life!"
—Fallen Angel Reviews

Love Means… Freedom

"Mr. Grey has, once again, brought to life compelling characters with whom readers can identify and about whom we can care deeply. This is one of those books best read snuggled up in a cozy, favorite chair while the wind howls outside."
—Whipped Cream Erotic Romance Reviews

Bottled Up

"Andrew Grey continues to stun me with his endearing storytelling."
—Two Lips Reviews

http://www.dreamspinnerpress.com

Books by
ANDREW GREY

THE BOTTLED UP STORIES
Bottled Up
Uncorked
The Best Revenge
An Unexpected Vintage
A Shared Range

THE CHILDREN OF BACCHUS STORIES
Children of Bacchus
Thursday's Child
Child of Joy

THE LOVE MEANS… STORIES
Love Means… No Shame
Love Means… Courage
Love Means… No Boundaries
Love Means… Freedom

A Taste of Love

All published by
DREAMSPINNER PRESS

Hugs &
Love.

Andrew Grey

A TASTE OF Love

ANDREW GREY

Dreamspinner Press

Published by
Dreamspinner Press
4760 Preston Road
Suite 244-149
Frisco, TX 75034
http://www.dreamspinnerpress.com/

A Taste of Love
Copyright © 2010 by Andrew Grey

Cover Art by Reese Dante   http://www.reesedante.com
Cover Design by Mara McKennen

ISBN: 978-1-61581-631-6

Printed in the United States of America
First Edition
November, 2010

eBook edition available
eBook ISBN: 978-1-61581-632-3

To the foodie in the family, Dominic.

Yes, for the last sixteen years
I have actually listened to all the talk
about the nuances of sauces,
the consistency of buttercream,
and just how well the Shiraz
goes with the roast duck.

This story is truly for you.

CHAPTER ONE

DARRYL loved spring, and it was definitely in the air. Pulling his front door closed, he looked up at the blue sky and inhaled deeply. The air smelled of pear blossoms, and as he walked toward the car, a breeze filled the air with white floating petals. Deciding it was too nice to drive, Darryl turned and began walking down the sidewalk, turning onto the main street of town. Heading toward the business district, he passed stately Victorian mansions, most turned into apartments, but many retaining the opulent look of a bygone era. As he continued walking, Darryl couldn't help looking between the buildings to catch glimpses of the old cemetery and its bronze statue marking the grave of Molly Pitcher. God, he loved this town. Carlisle, Pennsylvania, had been founded by William Penn in the mid-eighteenth century. As Darryl approached the square, he looked at the large church on the corner with its cherry tree in full bloom behind the sign that reminded everyone that George Washington had worshipped there in 1794.

He let his gaze travel around him as he waited for the light, looking up past the immense columns with scars from the Civil War, duly marked, to the clock on the old courthouse. As the light changed, he crossed the street and walked the remaining half block to his restaurant, pausing outside to look a few seconds.

Café Belgie was his dream. Darryl had spent almost a decade working in other people's kitchens until he'd managed to scrimp and save the money to open his own place. He'd chosen a Belgian-themed restaurant because that was what he loved. Good, simple food with a certain flair. Besides, it gave him an excuse to carry the most wonderful selection of beer. Stepping to the door, he gazed one last time up the street at the trees filled with blossoms that rained down on the sidewalk.

Reaching for the door, he tugged lightly, not at all surprised that it opened easily despite the closed sign in the window. His pastry chef, Maureen, was already at work—like always, the first one there.

"If you think I'm going to take that shit, you're crazy, woman!" Sebastian, one of his servers, was upset, and his voice carried out into the street and drowned out the sound of traffic. "I'm not working the lunch shift alone. Darryl will just have to call someone in to help." God, the man could wail, and Darryl felt it like fingernails on a chalkboard.

Darryl stepped inside and let the door close with a thud as he saw Maureen throw her hands up and walk back into the kitchen. "It's a Wednesday and lunch is always slow, so what are you bitching about?" Darryl said, raising his voice, his good mood from the walk vanishing in an instant. "Quit being such a drama queen and get ready for service." He walked to the server's station. "You'll need more napkins folded, and make sure all the tables are ready." Darryl glared at the tall, almost elegant young man. The customers loved him and he was a great server, but his attitude sucked. "You're not going to slough off the work on someone else so you can make all the tips."

Darryl watched as Sebastian put on his innocent face, pushing out his lower lip in a pout that would have been cute if Darryl hadn't already known it was completely fake. "But Darryl, we've already got a reservation for a party of ten."

Fuck, he was adorable when he did that. And if Darryl hadn't already experienced a Sebastian tantrum at least once a week for the past three months, he might have been tempted to take the man home and fuck him within an inch of his life. Darryl had no doubt Sebastian was very talented, if even half of what he said was true, but it just wasn't worth the aggravation. "Then you'd better get the table set up and ready." He checked his watch. "We open in less than an hour, and you're going to move your ass." Darryl looked down his nose. "That is, if you want a shot as the front-of-house manager." Without another word, Darryl walked through the dining room, looking at everything as he did, checking that the tables were straight, floors clean, even that the pictures on the wall weren't crooked, before entering the kitchen, his domain.

Maureen was still fuming as she walked back to her workstation, slamming one of the cooler doors. "The little shit," she muttered as she cut butter into one of the mixers and turned it on.

"What'd he do now?" Darryl asked as he took off his shirt and shrugged into his chef's coat before getting to work making the sauces and turning on the grill. He had a lot to do in an hour. Checking that the fryers were clean, he turned them on to get up to temperature. He heard the kitchen door open and close. "Morning, Kelly," he said without looking up.

"Morning, Darryl." She got her coat on and went right to work. "I'll get the fries cut and precooked. I made curry ketchup and the mayonnaise last night just before I left, so we should be good."

"Wonderful." Sometimes he wondered what he'd do without her. He gave his prep cook a smile, then turned his attention to Maureen. "You gonna tell me what's eating you or make me guess?"

"He"—she tilted her head toward the dining room—"tried to sweet-talk me into filling the salt and peppers for him. Seems he forgot to do it at the end of his last shift, and when I told him no, he got all pissy. Damn queen." Darryl glanced up and saw her shake her head. "If he wasn't otherwise good at his job, I'd kick his ass into traffic."

"I know," Darryl said. He continued working, wishing Sebastian would show the rest of the staff the same courtesy he showed the customers. The kid was like a switch, throwing himself on "happy" whenever he smelled a tip.

But Sebastian was no match for Maureen. The woman might be small and slight, but she didn't take crap from anyone. She'd been Darryl's best friend for years. Maureen had worked at the bakery that supplied the desserts to the first restaurant he'd worked in all those years ago, and when he decided to open Café Belgie, there was no one else he'd wanted making his desserts, particularly since she had the flair to make authentic European-style desserts that complemented his food. "There are times I want to wring his neck"—Darryl looked up at his kitchen staff—"but if he'd tone it down just a bit, he'd be fantastic." Darryl knew it was true, he just wasn't sure Sebastian was capable of doing it. That was what the young man needed to prove to him as well as to the rest of the staff.

"Are you really considering giving him the front of the house?" Kelly asked as she fed potatoes through the cutter while the first batch was cooking. They were known for their traditional *pommes frites*; anywhere else they might have been called French fries, but not in Darryl's restaurant! They were cooked twice—once to cook them through and once to crisp them—and nobody, including Darryl, could do it as well as Kelly.

"Only if he steps up." Darryl continued working, finishing the preparations for lunch. "And only if you agree as well."

The kitchen got silent as the other two stopped moving. "Are you kidding?" Maureen asked as she went back to filling chocolate cylinders with mint mousse. "You want us to decide?"

"We'll all decide." Darryl had just hit on this idea, and it just might get Sebastian to change his attitude. "You can feel free to let him know that as well."

"Damn, boss," Kelly said, laughing over the crackle of the fresh oil, "you're one smart cookie."

The sound of another screech from out front made all of them laugh, and Maureen set down her pastry bag. With a smile of sheer delight, she left the kitchen to have a talk with Sebastian. The door swung outward and then back in, and Darryl heard a "What!?" at the top of Sebastian's lungs. The door settled to a close before banging open, hitting the stops and swinging back toward a glaring Sebastian, who dodged it easily. "You're letting them… you're not serious?"

"Of course I am, so drop the diva act and step up." Darryl checked his watch. "We open in fifteen minutes, so make sure you're ready." Darryl almost laughed when he saw the pout again, followed by a tilt of the head. "Flirting won't help, either. It's time you put up or shut up." Darryl glared at him and saw Sebastian's face firm and his back straighten. "You need to prove you can do the job." Letting his expression soften, Darryl stepped from behind the line to where Sebastian stood near the doors. "I know you've got what it takes, you just have to prove it to all of us."

Sebastian looked at him, and then his eyes traveled to Kelly and Maureen, who, to their credit, looked serious and businesslike, even though Darryl knew they were both delighted as hell that they had something that would keep Sebastian in line, if only for a while. "I will, Darryl." With nothing more, Sebastian turned and left the kitchen.

Just before opening, Darryl made one final inspection of the dining room. Every table looked perfect. Utensils and glasses set, menus ready, and the vases filled with fresh flowers. It looked great—up to the standards he set. "You ready?" he asked Sebastian, before propping the door open and putting out the specials board. Walking back through the restaurant, he turned and saw the first customers already walking in and sitting down.

The lunch service was unexpectedly busy, to say the least. The kitchen filled with the sounds of work: orders being called, questions answered over the sounds of cooking, and banging dishes. To the uninitiated it might look and sound like complete chaos, but to Darryl and his staff, it was nearly as graceful as a ballet. "That's the last order," Sebastian called as he stuck his head inside, and Darryl could hear his server's breathlessness. The few times he'd had a second to peek, he'd seen the customers running Sebastian ragged. Leaving Kelly to finish the last order, he walked out front and saw Carter, one of the bussers, clearing the tables as Sebastian helped him. The dishwashing area would be busy for another hour, but everything had gone well.

"Darryl, we really need to think about hiring another server at least part time," Sebastian said as he approached him. "Lunch is getting busier, and I can't handle it alone."

Darryl smiled. "I think so, yes." Sebastian looked shocked, and Darryl let his smile increase. Maybe he could turn this into a lesson. "See, you get what you want when you ask, not shout."

"So you'll do it?"

Darryl nodded. "But you'll need to train them and take them under your wing."

"Then I have the job?" Sebastian's eyes widened hopefully.

Darryl let his smile fall. "I didn't say that. But training and managing wait staff, bussers, and even the dish room are all part of the job." Darryl softened his face. "You did good today, but waiting tables is what you know. Let's see how you learn new things." The front door opened, and more patrons entered. Darryl cut the conversation short and returned to the kitchen.

"I'm heading out," Maureen called as she gathered her things. "The desserts for tonight are all set, and you just need to sauce and plate them." Maureen opened the cooler door, the smell of mint wafting out as she showed him the trays of dessert and the squeeze bottles of sauce.

"They look marvelous and smell even better." She smiled at the compliment and bumped his hip.

"Flattery will get you everywhere." She closed the cooler door and smacked his shoulder. "Get out of here for a while and enjoy the sun," she called as she hurried out the back door.

"Yeah, boss," Kelly piped up with a smile. "I can handle things for a while. I just have to finish the orders for that last table." Darryl knew she'd been itching to show him that she could do more. After taking a peek to make sure there weren't many people out front, he turned back to her.

"Okay. The show's yours." He noted her smile. "But call me if you have any problems. I won't be too long." She agreed, and he left the kitchen, walking through the dining room, out the front door, and into the spring sunshine. He needed this desperately; so many of his days were spent inside, arriving before the sun was up and leaving long after dark. The restaurant required long hours, but he loved it. Turning around, he looked up at his baby. The brick looked clean, and the windows sparkled. Sitting down on the bench in front, he turned so he could watch people walking along the sidewalk. He waved at the man from the men's clothing store who was also taking a break, enjoying the sunshine. Darryl thought he was going to come and say hello, but a young man entered his store, and Darryl watched as he followed.

A few minutes later, the young man walked out again and walked into the next store, coming out again a few minutes later and repeating the process. Again and again, the man walked from business to business, and as he got closer, Darryl saw his face fall a little more each time. He must be looking for a job, and Darryl knew that in this market, they were hard to come by. As the man got closer, Darryl could see that he was younger than he'd thought, and he knew that eventually it would be his turn to be asked.

Sure enough, a few minutes later, he saw the young man walk past him and go into the restaurant. He really was young, but Darryl had to admire his determination. He came out a minute later and walked over to him. "Sir, the man inside said I needed to talk to you." The voice was soft and rhythmic, and damn young. "I'm looking for a job, and the man inside said you might be hiring." The hopeful look in his deep eyes tugged at Darryl's heart.

"We might." Darryl looked the young man in the eye and felt as though he'd been punched in the gut at the jolt that went through him. "What experience have you had?"

"Not much, I'm afraid." Darryl saw him shuffle from foot to foot. "We moved here a few months ago, and I need a job real bad. I'll work hard, real hard." The earnestness in his voice caught Darryl's attention, even as the eyes bored into him with a pleading look. "I'll do anything you need, wash dishes, sweep floors, clean tables."

"The only position I have open right now is for a part-time server," Darryl replied, and saw the hope in the man's eyes lift, but it was the fear tinged with desperation that made Darryl curious.

"I can do that. I'm a fast learner!" His eyes brightened, and he bounced slightly on the balls of his feet. "All I need is a chance." God, the energy and excitement were catching, and the kid's enthusiasm was encouraging.

"Okay. I'll give you a chance." Hell, enthusiasm and energy had to count for something. "Come inside and you can fill out an application." Darryl stood up and the kid followed him like a happy puppy, his feet barely touching the ground. Darryl felt eyes on him and turned around. "By the way, how old are you?"

"Twenty-one," the young man answered quickly, and Darryl breathed a sigh of relief. At least serving alcohol wouldn't be an issue.

He went right to his small office off the kitchen, fishing through the files for the proper forms. "Fill these out, and I'll need to see your identification and social security card." Darryl handed him the forms and the kid's hand shook, he had so much excited energy.

Darryl sat back and watched as, looking at the top of the form, *William* filled out the application. "Do you go by Will?" he asked, trying to make him a little more comfortable.

"Everybody calls me Billy." He looked up and a smile split his face, radiating through the room. Damn, the kid was adorable, and as Darryl watched, he leaned forward in the chair and shrugged off his jacket. Long black hair flowed from beneath it, shimmering in waves to his shoulders. If he were a girl, he could have been a supermodel. The man was stunning with that long hair, big eyes, and lips…. Darryl dragged his eyes away and concentrated on the forms that Billy handed him.

"I'm Darryl Hansen." He held out his hand, figuring introductions were in order. "I'm the owner and chef." He glanced at the form. "And you're Billy Weaver." Darryl checked over the form, and everything looked in order. Checking over his identification, Darryl smiled. "We'll try you out tomorrow during lunch. Be here at ten and I'll introduce you to Sebastian. He'll show you around, and you'll work with him for a few days until you get a feel for how we do things."

Billy grasped Darryl's hand, breaking into another smile as he pumped it vigorously. "Thank you. I won't let you down. I promise." Billy grabbed his worn jacket and turned around, treating Darryl to a peek at the kid's stunning backside. "I'll see you tomorrow, Mr. Hansen."

Darryl swore Billy's feet never hit the ground as he rushed toward the door to the dining room, turning around to wave before disappearing. Darryl found himself watching the door, completely lost in thought.

"Darryl!" Hearing his name, he turned to Kelly, who was standing in his doorway. "Geez, where were you?" She didn't wait for an answer, putting a plate in front of him before plopping into the only other chair. "I think we're done for a while, so I made you something to eat." Darryl barely heard her, his mind still on the kid—er, Billy. "Earth to Darryl, are you there?"

"Sorry." He pulled his mind back to the present. "What's this?"

"I made it for you. Tell me what you think." Kelly looked pleased as Darryl examined the plate. The presentation was good, and he sniffed at the food. The aroma was enticing without being overpowering. Picking up the utensils, he cut a bite and tasted it. "Very nice. A variation on veal Milanese." The breading was crisp but not too heavy, thin with a nice mouth-feel.

"Yes, except I breaded it, and instead of frying it, I sautéed it in a very little oil to keep it lighter." Kelly watched as he cut off another bite. Popping it into his mouth, he let the flavor run free. "Do you like it?"

"Yes. We'll need to refine the process, but this could definitely work on the menu as a special. Let's talk about it tomorrow; you can think about what you'd like to serve with it."

Kelly practically squealed with delight as she hopped out of the chair, and Darryl smiled as he continued eating, his mind returning unbidden to a vision of Billy. Jesus, he needed to stop that. Yes, the kid fascinated him. He had energy and was absolutely adorable, but he was way too young. And besides, Darryl had a hard and fast rule: he never dated anyone he worked with. He was the boss, and that could open a kettle of worms he wasn't interested in exploring. But damn, the kid seemed to push all his buttons. "Maybe it's just been too long," he muttered to himself. Darryl tried to remember the last time he'd spent time with anyone and he realized he couldn't. "Fuck, it's been forever since I had any kind of sex that didn't involve my right hand."

He heard a soft knock and looked up to find himself looking again into Billy's big, expressive eyes. "I forgot to ask how I should dress." Billy looked nervous, and from the look of the clothes he was wearing, Darryl surmised that he probably didn't have much.

"Wear black pants, and I'll give you a few Café Belgie shirts that you can wear when you're working." Billy looked relieved and flashed Darryl another smile that raced through him.

"Okay, thank you."

Again, Darryl watched him go and had to remind himself of his rule. The kid looked so young and innocent. Darryl usually liked his men more experienced, but there was something about Billy that got his attention, and it scared the fuck out of him. Shaking his head, he forced himself to finish his lunch. Nothing was going to happen, no way, no how. Besides, Sebastian was going to train him, and Darryl intended to keep as far away from the kid as possible. His first job had been in a kitchen with a very talented chef who had dated all the women who worked for him. What a mess that had been for everyone. No, he wouldn't put himself in that position, even for a man as attractive as Billy. *Jesus, I'm doing it again.* Finishing his lunch, he took the plate to the dish room and got to work. That would take his mind off that bright smile, radiant hair, and tiny, tight butt. "Jesus Christ!" He swore at himself.

"Is something wrong?" Kelly asked, concerned.

"No," Darryl lied, forcing his mind onto his work.

CHAPTER TWO

THE kitchen door opened, and Darryl looked up from behind the line and saw Billy peeking over the shelf. "Someone wants their steak frites with regular butter instead of the herb butter, is that okay?"

"Of course." Darryl felt his mouth go dry as Billy smiled at him and handed him the note to go with the ticket. "You can just enter it on the computer. You don't have to come back to tell me whenever you have a special request." The smile faded just a little bit, and Darryl found himself wanting to put that smile back. It just brightened everything. "You're doing fine. Don't worry. You'll get the hang of it."

Billy nodded a little and turned around, leaving the kitchen, and Darryl found himself watching the door until a steak flared on the grill and he returned his attention to where it should be. He heard Kelly snicker a little, and she turned away from him, but he glared at her nonetheless. She must have seen him anyway. "Come on, boss, it's funny."

"What is?" He turned the steak, thankful it wasn't burned. "I need two frites and a Niçoise salad," he said, looking ahead to the next ticket.

"Okay, chef," Kelly replied with a knowing smile, dropping the frites into the fryer and starting on the salad with practiced ease.

"You have something to say?" Darryl glanced up from his work, adding another steak to the grill and setting up two orders of mussels to steam.

"Nothing. It's just that every time Billy comes in here, you forget what you're doing. It's funny." Kelly placed the salad on the pickup station and pulled out the frites, letting them drain before transferring them to the paper cones. "If I didn't know better, I'd say you were sweet on him."

Darryl saw her bat her eyes at him teasingly, and he swatted her with his towel. "I am not. I just want to make sure he's doing well. It's his first week, after all." He hoped Kelly bought the explanation, because while what he said was true—he did want him to do well—fuck, the kid could scramble his concentration with just a simple smile. It had been a long time since anyone had that kind of effect on him. He liked it, sort of, but there was no way he was going to act on it. He just had to deal with it.

Finishing the orders, he wiped the edges of the plates and pressed the button to tell the server that their order was ready. Billy bustled into the kitchen, picking up the plates and hurrying out again, taking a second to flash him another smile. Darryl closed his eyes and pushed away the images that flooded his brain. Billy was grateful for the job and happy to be working, that was all. Kelly's chuckles cut through his thoughts, and he gave her a final glare before returning his attention to where it should be, on his food. "Keep it up and I won't put your dish on special tonight." He tried to sound menacing, but Kelly just smiled, seeing right through him.

"Come on, Darryl," he heard Maureen interject from the pastry station. "Billy's been working here three days and he's already got you wrapped around his little finger," Maureen said with a hint of laughter in her voice. "If you ask me, it's about time someone caught your attention. I was beginning to think the pipes were clogged or something." Both Maureen and Kelly laughed, and Darryl scowled at them.

"My pipes are just fine." Damn it, he'd said that way too loud, and he looked up, thankful the door to the dining room was closed. Both women returned to their stations, heads down, shoulders bouncing, and he knew they were laughing. He was never so thankful for anything in his life as when the printer started spitting out orders. "Need two more frites and a Caesar." Darryl ripped off the ticket, and another came right behind. "Seems your mousse is a hit, I need three of them," he said to Maureen as he began preparing the main dishes.

"Billy sells more dessert than anyone I've ever seen," Maureen commented as she went to the refrigerator, pulling out three decorative glasses filled with a creamy chocolate and garnishing them with whipped cream and strawberries.

"It's those eyes," Kelly replied, the words passing around Darryl as he tried to concentrate on his work. "Can you imagine saying no to him?" Kelly stopped what she was doing, looking at Maureen. "Would you like some chocolate mousse?" Darryl glanced up from his pointed effort to ignore the two of them, sighed in frustration while shaking his head, and forced his attention back on his work, to no avail. "Every woman out there says yes, thinking about what she'd like to do with that mousse."

An image of Billy flashed in his mind, smooth skin, big eyes, chocolate mousse streaking his…. A clang as his spoon hit the floor pulled him back to the present, and both women howled. "You're way too easy." Maureen thumped him on the back before doubling over with laughter. Darryl growled and picked up the spoon, tossing it into the sink. Yanking open the stainless steel drawer, he grabbed another and went back to work, growling as the other two turned back to their stations, still snickering.

The lunch service wound down, and Darryl got Kelly started on the prep for dinner while he whipped up something for lunch. Everyone worked long hours and always through the times that "normal" people ate lunch, so Darryl tried to create something interesting each day for the staff and himself between the lunch and dinner service. As he was finishing, the back door opened. "Hey, boss!"

"Should have known." Darryl grinned at the newcomer. "Julio, you always show up when we're getting ready to eat."

"Can't today." He patted his stomach. "Maria says I'm getting fat and put me on a diet. She made me promise, Papi."

"What started this?" Darryl dished up the food, and Kelly and Maureen helped him carry it to the back table in the dining room, with Julio following behind.

"She watched some show on television, and now she has it in her head that I'm going to die and leave her alone." Julio shook his head and turned back toward the door. "I'm going to start in the kitchen and get away from temptation." The door swung closed behind him, and Darryl took his chair, with the others taking a seat as well, Billy sitting right across from him, of course.

"I'm thinking of using this as a special, so I want your honest opinion." Dishing up, he placed a piece of chicken on each plate along with vegetables and herbed potatoes, adding just a dash of sauce. The plates were passed, and everyone began to eat and offered their opinion or asked questions. "This isn't the presentation I'll use," he explained in answer to a question from Sebastian, who was obviously enjoying his lunch.

Kelly kept eating but knitted her brow slightly. "I love the chicken, and the herbed potatoes are great, but I think the sauce needs just a tad more zing."

Darryl took a bite himself. He'd tasted each ingredient as he was making them, but this was the first time he'd been able to taste them together, and she was right, the sauce did need a little something else. "It does, but I'll have to think what's missing."

"Wuit," Billy mumbled, and Darryl looked over at him as he swallowed and started again. "I think it might need something sweet, like fruit." Every head at the table looked to Billy, and Darryl saw him try to sink in his chair, the young man's pale face turning red.

"He's right." Darryl smiled across the table, noticing that Billy's plate was empty. Hell, the thing practically sparkled, it was so clean. "I was going to ask how you liked it otherwise," Darryl said as he reached for the kid's plate, giving him another helping, and Billy tucked right in, eating almost furiously. "But I think I got my answer." Darryl chuckled at the implicit compliment. Nothing said that someone liked your food as much as people who ate like there was no tomorrow. And Billy took that one step further.

Darryl continued eating, watching as Billy cleaned his plate again in near-record time. Thinking over the last few days, Darryl noticed that Billy always seemed to eat that fast, only slowing down once he'd eaten at least an initial portion. Conversation around the table continued as various discussions of food, customers, tipping gripes, and even a few weird restaurant stories circulated. But Darryl heard almost none of it as he watched Billy. The kid was so thin, and it made Darryl wonder.

"So is my veal the special for tonight?" Kelly asked excitedly, pulling him out of his thoughts.

"Yup, so you better make sure everything's ready so you can go over it with the waiters before you leave." She looked at him wide-eyed. "This is your dish, so you need to take the lead." Kelly smiled and nodded, pushing back her chair and taking her dishes with her, a spring in her step.

Something prickled at the pack of Darryl's mind. "Billy, how'd you know about the sauce?"

He shrugged, looking at Darryl with those big eyes as wide as saucers. "Just know what I like, I guess." He looked down at the table. "The stuff you make is real good; I just thought it needed fruit." Darryl looked at the kid's plate, and it was clean again—spotless, as a matter of fact. How he could eat so fast was beyond him. "I need to help Sebastian with the napkins and stuff." Billy stood up and picked up his dishes, taking Darryl's as well, and scuttled away to the dish room. The others at the table had largely finished and were getting up as well, filtering away and back to work.

Darryl heard the phone ring once, and a few seconds later, Kelly came out of the kitchen. "That was Janet. She's got the flu and can't come in tonight."

"Shit!" Darryl pulled the napkin off his lap and tossed it on the table. "Billy." He saw him come out of the back, carrying a tub of clean napkins. "Can you work tonight? We're a little short."

"Can I use the phone to check?" He sounded so tentative, like he was suddenly preoccupied with something else.

"Of course." Darryl got up and went back in the kitchen as Sebastian cleared and prepared the table they'd just used for the dinner service. Maureen steered her boss to the coolers and explained the desserts before saying her goodbyes and leaving. Kelly was hard at work on her preparations, and Julio was deep in the freezer doing the weekly inventory and cleaning.

Billy walked in. "I can stay, but not too late." He looked uncomfortable adding the last part, but Darryl understood.

"It's not a problem. If you can stay through the rush, we should be able to manage from there." Billy smiled again. "See Sebastian, and he can tell you all about the dinner service."

"Okay, sir," Billy answered, returning to the dining room, the door swinging behind him, and Darryl got back to work, trying not to think too hard about his young server.

The afternoon went by quickly, and all too soon the dinner service was in progress, the pace near frantic. Kelly had left after the first few of her specials were met with rave reviews from the customers, and Julio had taken over as Darryl's backup.

"I need to go home now, if that's okay." Darryl looked up from the grill and saw Billy bouncing nervously on his heels.

"Of course. You did really good today, thank you." Darryl watched out of the corner of his eye as Billy got his jacket.

"'Night," Billy said as he opened the back door.

Darryl looked up and saw Billy bend down to pick up what looked like a to-go container, and then the door closed. For a second, he wondered what Billy could be taking home, and then a group of orders came in and he continued with the service.

Business continued to slow down during the final hours until closing. A number of people came in after dinner, but they mostly sat and had a beer or two. One of the things that had been great for business was the selection of authentic Belgian beer that they had on tap. People came in a couple times a week just for a beer and to watch a game or talk.

At closing time, he and the staff cleaned the kitchen, and the tables were largely set for the following day. Closing and locking the front door, they finished the last of their tasks and everyone said their good-nights. Darryl, nearly always the last to leave, turned out the lights and locked the back door, walking to his car. The day had been sunny but cold, so he was thankful he'd had the foresight to drive. Walking to his car, he climbed in and headed for home, his mind winding down and his thoughts wandering. Like they had done over the last few days, they quickly turned to Billy. He didn't know what it was, but something about the kid fascinated him.

"Shit!" Darryl hit the brake in his distraction over Billy, and the car behind him laid on the horn. Getting his attention back on the road, he continued driving, trying to concentrate. But it was hard as thoughts kept scrolling through his head. Billy had known what was wrong with his sauce right away and had told him so without hesitation or doubt. That was extraordinary, since Darryl doubted Billy had ever been around fine cooking before. Hell, the kid had asked him earlier in the week why there were two forks on the table. His young server was an enigma, that was for sure. As he pulled up to the front of his house, Darryl found his brow furrowing as he remembered that he'd thought he saw Billy carrying a container out of the restaurant. He didn't think he'd steal food, but he made a mental note to check the inventory in the morning just to be sure.

Getting out, he dragged himself up the walk to his front door and went inside, dropping his keys in the bowl and dragging himself up the stairs. Stripping off his clothes, he turned on the water and stepped beneath the shower, his body protesting every movement while his mind played images of Billy. "What the fuck is wrong with me?" Darryl stepped under the water, trying not to think of his raven-haired server with eyes that danced and a smile that lit the room. "Jesus, ya perv. The kid's way too young and obviously as innocent as hell." Darryl washed quickly and rinsed before turning off the water. Stepping out, he dried himself and collapsed into bed. He thought about jerking off but knew he'd probably think of Billy, and he just didn't want to go there.

CHAPTER THREE

DARRYL woke in his bed, alone, the way he always did. Pushing back the covers, he groaned softly as he sat up, his hands on his head to keep it from throbbing. He felt like he'd spent the night drinking, but that wasn't it. Every time he fell asleep, Billy's face kept playing behind his eyes—and it wasn't always just his face. All night long, over and over, his mind kept playing the things he'd like to do to his young waiter, and no matter how many times he told himself that Billy was way too young for him, his mind and body just weren't listening.

Getting off the bed, he stood up and padded to the bathroom. Opening the medicine cabinet, he grabbed the can of shaving cream and squirted a dab in his hand. Holding it in his palm, he found himself looking in the mirror. When he closed his eyes, Billy's face appeared in front of him, and the hand with the shaving cream slid lower. Darryl hissed as the cool foam surrounded his length and squeezed between his fingers. Keeping his eyes closed, he let the images that had been playing all night have free reign. Billy, naked, eyes piercing, skin shining, reached out to him. Darryl could almost feel his touch and began to stroke slowly, fingers working over his length, his hips moving slightly. The image knelt in front of him, and suddenly his hand was Billy's lips, his cock disappearing into his hot, wet throat, and Darryl heard a groan echo from outside himself.

The imaginary Billy hummed around his dick, and in his mind, Darryl looked down as Billy began stroking himself, the humming and excitement building. Darryl could almost hear it echoing off the walls as he increased the speed of his hips, thrusting into his hand-turned-Billy's-mouth. The humming in his head got louder, and he increased the pressure. In his mind, Billy was taking him deep and hard, and Darryl thought he was going to lose his balance. Instead, he almost began to float, his imagination and endorphins taking him on a flight that was almost too good to be true.

He could almost feel Billy's hair between his fingers as Darryl's hips snapped, and he thrust deep into Billy's mouth. His body reacted in a big way, balls drawing close in, knees shaking, head throbbing, as he felt his release begin at his toes and jet from him, the walls echoing his cries.

The Billy in his mind faded, and slowly, Darryl opened his eyes, looking down. He was a complete and utter mess. There was shaving cream all over his crotch, his hands were covered with cum and cream, white blotches covered the bathroom rug, and he could barely stand up, let alone see straight. Stepping back, he leaned against the wall and let his hand fall away, breathing heavily. Jesus, he'd have thought he'd feel better, but he didn't. He had to stop this obsession with Billy. Somehow, some way, it had to end. He could terminate him, but the thought made him feel lower than low. Why should Billy have to suffer because he couldn't keep himself under control? No, he'd just have to deal with it. Pushing himself off the wall, he reached for a washcloth and began cleaning himself up. When he was done, he wrapped the cloth in the rug, throwing them in the laundry before shaving properly and washing up.

Leaving the bathroom, he dressed and walked into the kitchen, pouring himself a cup of life from the coffeemaker—God bless whoever had invented timers—and walked outside to the front steps to pick up the paper. He sat at the kitchen table, sipping his coffee and reading, for an hour until it was time to go into work, his mind quiet and unperturbed for the first time since he'd hired Billy.

ANDREW GREY

Finishing his morning ritual, he put his cup in the sink and threw the paper into the recycling. Opening his front door, he stepped out and dashed down his walk, dodging raindrops as he scurried into the car and drove away.

He parked in his usual space and walked inside. The restaurant was quiet for a change, no drama and no noise. He heard soft sounds of work coming from the kitchen and decided to take a few extra minutes in the dining room. The tables were set and ready, and the floor shone. Looking around, he smiled when he saw the colorful Belgian soccer jerseys hanging near the ceiling. He'd scoured the Internet for just the right colors, and all the teams had to be Belgian. He'd even managed to get a few team flags. Not only were the flags and jerseys colorful, they helped absorb sound and make the restaurant quieter and more conducive for talking. When he'd first opened, it had been way too loud.

"Morning, Mr. Hansen." Darryl turned around and saw Billy coming in from the kitchen, smiling brightly as he set down the tub of napkins. "Did you have a good night?"

The image from that morning of Billy on his knees flashed in his mind, and Darryl began to cough. "Yes, I did. Thank you."

"Are you okay?" Billy got a glass of water from behind the bar and rushed over.

Darryl swallowed the water, getting hold of himself. "Thank you." Jesus, fuck, one smile and a simple question from the kid and he couldn't keep his filthy mind out of the gutter. Without looking, Darryl excused himself and almost ran to the safety of his kitchen.

"What the hell's gotten into you?" Maureen scolded as he came in the kitchen. "You look about as guilty as someone who just ran over a dog." Darryl watched as she scowled at him. "You didn't, did you?"

"No. I did not hit a dog. God, Mo, where do you come up with this shit?"

She pursed her lips, looking him over. "Then what's been wrong with you the last few days? You're jumpy and all twitchy; it isn't good." Maureen began adding sugar to her mixture and turned on the mixer.

Darryl looked around. "Is Kelly here?"

"No, it's her day off. She did most of the prep last night for you." Maureen pointed to the note on the board. "You know that. What's gotten into you?"

Darryl motioned her to follow him, and she stopped the mixer and followed him to the back hall. "I can't stop thinking about Billy. Last night I had dreams about him. Every time I closed my eyes, I saw his face, his…." Darryl swallowed, uncomfortable talking about this with her but not sure who else he could talk about it with. "Every time I see him, I get… excited."

Maureen laughed. "I don't understand the problem. It's okay to like him."

Darryl huffed and saw one of Maureen's stray hairs blow in his breath. "He's way too young, and he works for me. I just can't be interested in him."

Maureen shook her head. "The funny thing is, we don't get to choose who catches our attention or makes our heart sit up and take notice." She smiled indulgently. "You've spent all the time I've known you working God knows how many hours and then working even harder to open this place. I don't know what you've done for sex all those years"—she held up her hands—"and Lord knows I don't want to, but I do know you've never had time for anyone else, not seriously."

"So what should I do?" He hated how lost he sounded.

"Do? Nothing. Just let nature take its course. You don't even know if Billy's interested. And you're right, he's young and an employee, but don't beat yourself up for your thoughts and fantasies; they're healthy, and they don't harm anyone." She smacked him on the arm. "Hell, if I told you about my fantasies, you'd probably die of embarrassment." She winked at him and walked back toward her work station. Darryl felt his mouth hanging open as he tried to figure out if Maureen fantasized about him. But damn, there was no way he was opening that kettle of worms. Some things he was just better off not knowing.

"Mr. Hansen?"

Darryl jumped in surprise and turned around, knowing Billy was right behind him. "Sebastian said I was to finish these napkins and sort the silverware, but he didn't tell me where he wanted me to put them."

"Oh, okay, I'll show you where they go." Darryl led him out front and showed him where everything went. "Where is Sebastian, anyway?" Darryl said to himself as he checked his watch. He should have been there by now.

"He called this morning and asked if I could help him out. He said he had a doctor's appointment and he didn't want stuff to sit. Since I live just down the street, it was easy for me to come in early."

Darryl returned to the kitchen to go back to work, but Maureen caught his eye and scowled at him lightly in the look he'd long ago learned to equate with confusion. "What is it, Darryl?"

He could feel his insides suddenly start to churn, and he wanted to run away. "I can't talk about it." He knew he was taking the coward's way out, but there was no way he could share this with anyone and be able to look them in the eye. Darryl felt his knees start to shake a little, and he thought he might lose his balance.

Maureen stepped closer. "There's more to this than Billy, isn't there?" Darryl nodded and took a deep breath. "We've known each other since we worked together at La Petite, and come to think about it, I've never seen you date anyone, or even express an interest in anyone." Maureen hugged him to her. "I don't know what happened to you, and you don't need to tell me until you're ready, if you ever are, but know that I won't judge you, no matter what." Darryl felt her rub his back gently, comforting him. "I know Billy's age has freaked you out for some reason, but he's an adult, and if he's interested, he'll let you know, and if he's not, then move on." Darryl said nothing; she was way too close to home for comfort. She let him go and stepped back. "Just relax and stop worrying and beating yourself up. Worry about your actions, not your thoughts."

"That's not what my parents always said," Darryl replied blandly. Hearing a door open and close reminded Darryl that other people were nearby, and he desperately wanted to end this conversation as soon as possible. He turned and walked to the board, pulling down Kelly's note and looking at it but not really seeing the words.

"If this is some sort of misplaced religious guilt," Maureen whispered behind him, and he turned, only to see her mad-as-hell look, something he always tried to avoid. Maureen was a great friend, but she could be a force to be reckoned with when she was mad. "I'll smack you into next week if you start believing all that 'lusting in your heart is going to send you to hell' crap. I know your dad believed all that shit, but it doesn't make it true, and you need to live your own life."

Darryl inhaled deeply and slowly released the breath. "I know, and if I forget, I know you'll be there to remind me."

"You're damn right!" She went back to her station and stopped the mixer, pulling off the bowl and getting back to work.

Picking up Kelly's note, he started reading through what she'd done and figuring out what he needed to finish. Somehow, he managed to concentrate on her note and went to work. Mechanically, he cut and chopped, filling the containers in the prep trays. For the longest time, he'd been able to push what had happened, what he'd done, to the back of his mind, but now it rushed forward, front and center. Leaving his station, he went to the sink and filled a glass with water, downing it in a few gulps.

"Mr. Hansen, should I open the doors?" He looked up and saw Billy standing in front of him, all smiles, with a happy glint in his eye.

Darryl checked his watch. "Is Sebastian here yet?" Billy shook his head. "How in hell can we open without all our servers?" He said it to the room but saw Billy's smile fade. *Fuck!* "I'm not mad at you. I'm just a little jumpy, I guess."

"Sebastian should be here any time. I can handle it." Billy thrust his chin out confidently. "It won't be busy for a while yet."

Darryl looked down at his station, anywhere but at those bright eyes and that cherubic face. "Thank you." He did his best not to watch Billy leave the kitchen but lifted his head anyway.

"I think that answered that question."

Darryl turned and glared at Maureen, his thoughts making him feel more bearish by the minute. "What question?" Darryl growled between his teeth, but Maureen just smiled in return.

"That boy smiles at everyone, but he only lights up like that when he's around you."

"Maureen, it doesn't matter. He works for me, and he's too young." He hoped he'd put some finality in his voice, but Maureen just scoffed and finished up what she was doing, putting the desserts in the cooler.

"Let's do lunch," she said with a smile as she moved to the prep station. On Kelly's day off, Maureen backed him up for lunch. While her skills weren't the same, she was a great cook and more than capable of supporting him. They always worked well together, and while she wasn't as intuitive as Kelly or Julio about what he was going to need, she always did her best.

The kitchen door opened, and Billy flew in, his eyes wide. "A party of fourteen just came in. I pushed tables together and got them seated, but we're filling up fast." His eyes were wide, and he sounded a little panicked.

A TASTE OF LOVE

"It's okay." Crises like this he could handle; it was his personal life that was a mess. "Do what Sebastian told you, and tell us if you get more people. Maureen or I can back you up until Sebastian gets here."

"But…," Billy stammered, and Darryl could see him bouncing on his feet.

Leaving his station, Darryl walked around to where Billy was standing. "You'll be fine." Without thinking, he placed his hands on Billy's shoulders. "Bring them water and take their drink orders. Then take their food orders and get them in the computer right away. When it comes time to serve, we'll help you." Those big eyes began to calm, and he could feel the nervousness slip away from the young man. Then Darryl became conscious of Billy's warmth under his hands, and a sweet, clean scent filled his nose. The kid was so appealing and absolutely beautiful with his round face and dimpled smile. Darryl pulled his hands away and stepped back. "You can do this. I know you can." Darryl couldn't look away from that sweet face. "Take your time, be accurate, and talk to them." Darryl smiled, wondering what else he should say.

"Billy, honey, here's a tray of waters." Maureen handed it to him. "If you get in trouble, just smile big and slow down." Billy took the tray and walked out of the kitchen.

Through the door, Darryl saw a group of ladies with presents on the table. "Looks like a lady's birthday party."

"Then he'll be just fine." Maureen returned to her station, and Darryl did the same. A short while later, the printer started, and Darryl got started on the orders, letting the work drive his other thoughts away. As the food orders began going out, Darryl saw orders start to appear with Sebastian's name on them, and he breathed a sigh of relief. Oh, he was pissed at the man for being late, but he was relieved that Billy was no longer alone.

The lunch rush slowed and then petered out. "God, that was something else," Maureen commented as she cleaned up around her station.

ANDREW GREY

"I'll clean up here if you'll check and update the inventory before you go? I've got to place the order for the weekend." It was no secret that he hated doing the inventory, so Maureen agreed, and he finished the cleanup of the area and cooked off the remainder of the lunch special for the staff lunch. Once he was done, he picked up the finished dishes and wandered out to the dining room, which looked as though a cyclone had hit it, and placed the food on the bar. Most of the tables needed to be cleaned. Billy had a tub, and he was gathering the dishes and hauling them back to the dish room. The bussers were cleaning tables as well, getting them ready for dinner. Sebastian was sitting at the bar, folding napkins and sorting silverware. Darryl walked over and sat next to him. "What happened to you? Billy got swamped, and you weren't here to help." He let a tinge of his aggravation color his voice.

"I had to go to the doctor, and they took forever. I tried to tell them I had to get to work, but they just went slower. I hurried over as soon as I could." It was obvious that Sebastian knew he'd left them in a jam. "I never expected them to take so long."

"Not that I'm happy you were late, but I'm glad you thought ahead and called Billy. He did great." He spoke loud enough to make sure Billy heard him. "Don't do it again," Darryl said, but his attention had shifted to Billy as he scurried about. The dining room was quickly resembling order again. The dishes were gone, and the tables, while empty, were at least clean. He saw Billy stop working and smile at him. Their eyes locked for a few seconds, and then he wasn't sure who blushed harder, himself or Billy. Darryl was the first to break eye contact, turning his attention to the food. "Help yourselves, guys." He saw Billy set down the bus tub and make a beeline for the bar, filling a plate and tucking in with his usual gusto. The others joined in as well, and by the time they'd all taken a serving, Billy had finished his and was getting more. "Like it?"

Billy smiled, his mouth full, and nodded vigorously as he continued eating. "It's really good."

"Did the birthday ladies treat you right?"

Billy blushed furiously. "They left me a hundred dollars!" he practically squealed, and Darryl thought he was going to do a little dance right there in the dining room. Then he moved closer. "The old lady at the head of the table, she's the one who left the tip. She pinched my butt when she left." Billy rubbed his rear unconsciously and turned even redder when Sebastian started laughing.

"I've been pinched, grabbed, and had women and men play 'drop the fork'. It's all part of the job."

Darryl furrowed his brow. "It is not part of the job!" The others stopped what they were doing and looked at him. "You are all trained professionals. You do your jobs in a clean, efficient manner. This isn't Hooters or the Playboy Club, it's Cafe Belgie, and I will not have my staff treated that way. Any of you." He glared at all of them. "The next time it happens, I want to know about it."

Darryl got up and took his plate with him, unsure why he was particularly angry. He wasn't upset with them. Servers took a lot of crap from customers, other servers, and even from him sometimes. They had a hard job, and he knew that crap like that went on, especially with the women, but with the guys as well. "Shit!" He dropped his dishes in the dish room, thankful that the guys were eating with the others, and headed right back to his office, closing the door. "Fuck." He plopped into his chair and held his head. If he were honest with himself, he knew why he was angry—that old bat had pinched Billy. Goddamnit, if anyone was going to do the pinching on that tight little butt, he wanted it to be him. "I have to get off this fucking guilt roller coaster somehow."

He heard a soft knock, and then the door opened. "I finished the inventory, and it's all good." Maureen handed him the clipboard and stepped inside.

"Thanks." He took the clipboard. "I'll see you tomorrow." She walked to him and kissed his cheek before leaving the office. Taking some time to himself, he finished some paperwork and updated the specials for the next few days on the restaurant website before returning to the kitchen.

"Hey, Julio, how's it going?" He saw his line cook cleaning beneath the kitchen fixtures. "Now that's what I like to see, a spotless kitchen."

"You already did most of it, so I figured I'd get ahead on the weekly jobs so we can get out of here early." Julio smiled as he continued working.

"Good man." Darryl was a stickler for cleanliness. His first chef had instilled that lesson hard and deep. "I'll be back to help in a little while."

"No problemo, Papi. I got it." The man straightened up. "But it might be a good time to ask for a raise." His face broke into a big, toothy grin.

"I just gave you one, last—" Darryl stopped and grinned. "What year is it, anyway?" They both laughed, and Julio went back to work. The raise thing was a standing joke between them. Darryl paid his people well, and as a consequence, he got the best people to work for him. Leaving the kitchen, he bumped into Billy, nearly knocking him down. "Sorry."

"I have to go, Mr. Hansen." He looked like he was in a hurry, his jacket already on.

"Okay. Thanks for covering, and no matter what that woman did, you did a great job and deserve every cent of that tip." Billy broke into one of those smiles, and Darryl's pants got tight. He had to put some distance between them. This kid was having an effect on him, one that he shouldn't and couldn't allow. "I'll see you tomorrow." Darryl kept his voice all business and walked behind the bar to check on supplies, anything to get himself under control. He heard the front door open and close. Looking up, he saw Billy disappear past the front windows. "Sebastian, we need glasses behind the bar."

"I know," Sebastian said as he approached the bar, "those birthday women drank raspberry Lambic like fish. I was just about to go get them. They should be clean." Darryl finished straightening things and heard the chink of glassware as Sebastian set a rack on the bar. "Did you give Billy something to take home?"

"No." That got Darryl's attention. "Why?"

"He was carrying a to-go container when he left." Sebastian began to put the glasses away.

"Goddamnit!" Darryl hurried back to the kitchen, grabbing his jacket form the office.

"Where you going, Papi?" Julio asked from near the kitchen floor.

"To fire a thief." As he said the words, he felt his heart sink. The kid had done so well and had such energy. "I'll be back in a few minutes." He'd had to do this before, and he hated it. "Get Sebastian to balance the register right away." Hurrying out front, he rushed through the dining room and out the front door. At least he knew those smiles and that wide-eyed innocent demeanor were just to throw him off.

Darryl stalked down the sidewalk, and ahead, he could see Billy waiting at the main intersection of town. Sure enough, he was carrying a white container. He could feel the anger and disappointment swell inside him. As he started to catch up, he saw the light change, and Billy crossed and continued down the sidewalk, pulling open the door of the Molly Pitcher Hotel and disappearing inside.

Darryl approached the front door and peered inside through the window. He didn't see Billy anywhere. Pulling open the door, he stepped inside the old, neglected building. The Molly had once been the premier hotel in town, but now, after decades of use and near neglect, it was a low-income residence. Looking around, Darryl spied the cubbyholes for mail behind the desk and saw the name Weaver on the cubbyhole marked 201. Darryl located the stairs and headed up. On the second floor, he followed the numbers toward the back of the building and knocked on the door.

Darryl waited just a few seconds and saw the door crack open and a familiar pair of eyes peek out. "Mr. Hansen." The door opened wider, and he saw the confused look on Billy's face. "What are you doing here?"

"Billy." Damn, he hated to do this here, but he really didn't have much of a choice. It was better to get this over with. "I have to let you go."

The door opened all the way, and Darryl saw that Billy hadn't even taken off his jacket. "But why?" he stammered weakly. "You said I did good and that I earned that tip." Darryl thought Billy was going to cry.

"It's because you stole food." Darryl looked into the small room and saw the to-go container sitting on the small table.

"I didn't steal anything." Billy straightened up and went inside, picking up the container and handing it to Darryl. Then the door closed with a click, and he found himself standing alone in the hallway. Not knowing what to do, Darryl absently opened the container.

"What the hell?" He looked inside and stared. There were a few small pieces of beef, a lump of mashed potatoes, half a dozen red potatoes, and a few vegetables. As he stared at the food wondering what was going on, he heard a door across the hall open, and two small heads poked into the hall. Quietly, they walked across the hall, one following the other, the leader stretching to open Billy's door. They couldn't have been any older than four or five.

"Biwwy, are you home?" The door opened, and Darryl saw Billy slumped against the wall just inside the door, his hands over his face, obviously crying. "Biwwy." Both boys raced to him, one crawling into his lap while the other hugged him around the neck. "Don't be sad." Billy pulled his hands down, tears running down his cheeks as he held and hugged both boys.

"Biwwy, I'm hungry," Darryl heard the child who'd been quiet up to now whisper softly.

"My tummy hurts," the other echoed, whining softly. He leaned his head against Billy's shoulder and started to cry softly. "You said if we were good, you'd bwing us food." Darryl got a glimpse of those big, sad eyes and turned away, feeling as though he was intruding.

The righteous indignation that had fueled Darryl's hurt and anger slipped away when he realized the meager amount of food he was holding in the container was meant for these kids. Darryl didn't know what to say, not that he could talk around the grapefruit in his throat. Slowly and quietly, he stepped forward and put a hand on the young man's shoulder. "Can I talk to you a minute?" He squeezed gently, barely able to get the words out.

Billy nodded and lifted himself off the floor. "Stay here, I'll be right back." They both nodded and stood huddled together near the wall, watching Billy as he stepped away. "Can I have the food? At least they'll have something to eat today," Billy said with a definite touch of anger in his voice.

Darryl handed him the container automatically. "Why didn't you tell me, or just ask?" He looked over Billy's shoulder at the boys, two pairs of eyes staring back at him. He noticed that both boys were holding their tummies and looked about two seconds from crying again.

Billy looked over his shoulder. "What was I supposed to tell you—that I've been starving and didn't know how I was going to feed my brothers?" He kept his voice low but ground out the words between his teeth. "Or maybe I was supposed to ask you if it was okay if I scraped food off other people's plates so they could eat." He pointed to the boys, tears streaking down his face even as his words carried an angry tone.

Darryl felt silly and ashamed. He'd never come face to face with hunger before, and looking into those small boys' faces, it was plain that they knew hunger, though they weren't much more than babies. Hell, this brought a lot of things into focus: Billy's prodigious appetite, the state of his clothes, and the relief that Darryl would provide them for work. His petty worries didn't matter so much now, and without thinking, he pulled the younger man into a hug and saw as the boys walked over, each clasping onto one of Billy's legs. "You're right, Billy. I'm sorry." The younger man felt so good in his arms that Darryl didn't want to let him go. Billy's heat slipped beneath his clothes and skin, while his clean, masculine scent went right to his heart. Darryl stepped back, afraid he'd overstepped, and took the container of food back, seeing Billy's hopeful expression fall. Kneeling down, he got to the little boys' eye level. "You want to come have lunch with me?" Both boys looked up at Billy, who nodded slowly, and then they both nodded vigorously, eyes wide.

Billy walked into the apartment, and Darryl followed and closed the door. It was a single, dingy room with a small table and two chairs, a dresser in the one corner covered with peeling paint, an old reclining chair in another corner, and two twin beds against the walls. The kitchen area was the remaining corner, with a small stove, sink, and refrigerator. Darryl could hardly believe his eyes and tried to keep his expression bland to show no reaction.

Billy opened one of the dresser drawers and pulled out two small jackets and handed them to the boys, who slipped them on. Darryl knelt down in front of the nearest little boy. "What's your name?"

"I Davey." A little hand pointed to his brother. "Dat's Donnie."

"They're my brothers," Billy added, as he slowly pulled on his own jacket.

"Well, Davey, are you ready to get some lunch?" Darryl asked. Davey's little head nodded with such vigor that Darryl thought he was going to hurt himself. "Then let's go eat." Darryl lifted the little boy in his arms, and two small hands locked around his neck. Darryl saw Billy lift Donnie, and Darryl led the way out of the apartment, with Billy closing and locking the door behind them.

They walked down the stairs and out onto the sidewalk, the little boy in his arms not really moving, just holding tight. Darryl didn't know what to say to Billy, so he kept quiet. He could hardly believe the turn of events. He'd gone to fire Billy and… shit, he had fired Billy. He cringed at himself. He'd jumped to conclusions and rather than ask him, he'd acted first, and now he felt like a complete ass. To top it off, he'd been agonizing over his attraction to Billy, and the kid had just been wondering where he was going to get the food to feed his brothers.

At the corner, they stopped and waited for the light. Billy turned to him. There was no hint of the smile that made Darryl all warm inside. All he saw was worry, misery, and fear. The light changed, and Billy stepped across the street. Darryl sped up and held the door as Billy walked inside. He may have acted like an ass, but he could make up for it now, or at least he could try.

CHAPTER FOUR

BILLY didn't know what the hell to think as he walked into Café Belgie. Darryl had fired him, and then not ten minutes later, he had Davey wrapped around his finger and was carrying his little brother out of their building and down the sidewalk to the restaurant. Once they were inside, Darryl had set Davey in a booth and told him that he'd be right back. Donnie still clung to Billy, not willing to let go, but Billy could see his big eyes taking everything in.

Darryl emerged from the kitchen carrying plates in one hand and a dish of crackers with bits of cheese in the other. "I didn't know what they'd like, but I figured this would be good to start." Darryl set the dish on the table in front of Davey, and the little boy reached in, shoving a cracker whole in his mouth, and started chewing. Donnie still seemed hesitant, so Billy sat down, and Donnie reached for a cracker, taking a bite before reaching for another. "I have some chicken fingers heating. I'll be right back." Darryl rushed back in the kitchen.

Sebastian came over and sat down across from Davey. "Who are you?" He gave the boy's tummy a little tickle.

"Davey, dat's Donnie." Davey spit out bits of cracker as he talked, pointing to his brother, who was shoving in the food with both hands. The kitchen door opened, and Darryl set down plates of chicken fingers with carrots and French fries.

"Sebastian, would you get two glasses of milk for the boys?" Darryl asked, and as Sebastian got up, he took his seat. Davey smiled up at him with a big cracker-crumb grin. Sebastian returned, setting down the glasses, and gave Donnie a tickle as well before returning to work.

Billy watched all this activity silently, still wondering what the hell was going on. "Mr. Hansen, why are you doing this?" The boys were now eating happily, and Billy let some of the tension ease from his body. If nothing else, at least Davey and Donnie were getting a good meal. Turning his attention back to his boss, er, ex-boss, he guessed, he waited for some sort of answer.

"Billy, we need to talk, but we can do that after the boys are done, okay?" Darryl stole a French fry from Donnie's plate, and the youngster glared at him before grabbing one for himself from the plate and shoving it into his mouth with a huge grin. "I have to check on some things for dinner, but I promise we'll talk just as soon as I'm done." Darryl touched his shoulder as he stood up, and Billy felt the same tingle he had when Darryl had hugged him, like somehow everything would be all right.

Darryl went into the kitchen, and Billy watched over the boys, making sure they didn't make too big a mess. Sebastian stopped back over and brought placemats and crayons. "Janet's mom called, and she'll be out for a few weeks. She picked up a case of mono somewhere. So can you work the dinner shift tonight?"

"I don't know." Billy looked at the kitchen door. Did he still have a job? Who was going to take care of the boys? He couldn't ask Mrs. Tadesco again. She was sweet, but Billy knew that long stretches watching the boys were hard on her.

"Hey, Sebastian." Darryl stuck his head in. "Where's Janet? Isn't she supposed to be here?" Sebastian got up and walked to where Darryl was standing. Billy watched as they talked, and then Darryl walked over to him, and Sebastian went back to work. "I know we need to talk, but I'm sorry for acting hastily, and if you want"—Darryl actually seemed a little nervous—"I'd like you to still work here."

Relief flooded through him, and he smiled and nodded his head, getting a smile back from Darryl. "I know you need someone to help tonight, but I don't have anyone to watch the boys." He looked over and saw both of them coloring and scribbling on the placemats, looking up at him every few minutes before returning to their drawings.

"Don't worry about that. They can play in my office. That way, they'll be close by, and we can check on them throughout the evening." Billy wasn't so sure how that was going to work, but he was grateful for Darryl's offer and found himself nodding as he looked into the man's brown eyes. Something about his boss drew him to the man, but he could never act on it—Darryl was his boss. The man was just being nice because he felt sorry for them.

Billy looked away from those puppy-brown eyes and saw Davey yawn, followed by Donnie. Being twins, they always did things together, and if one got sleepy, Billy knew the other wasn't far behind. Darryl reached into the booth, and Davey went right into his arms like he belonged there. As Darryl held his brother, Donnie put his head on his shoulder and yawned again, nearly half asleep. Darryl tilted his head toward the back room, and Billy lifted Donnie, following Darryl through the kitchen to the office in the back of the building.

"They can rest in here." Darryl pushed the door open, and Billy followed him inside. Darryl laid Davey on a futon, and Billy placed Donnie next to him, the two boys hugging each other. His boss pulled the throw from the back of the cushion and spread it over them before signaling to leave the room, cracking the door open behind them. "I've been considering getting rid of the futon. I used to sleep on it some nights when I was trying to get the restaurant opened," Darryl said softly as he led them back through the kitchen to the table in the dining room. "We have awhile before we open for dinner, and I thought we could have that talk now."

"Oh." Billy nodded as he sat in the booth.

"I don't want to pry." Darryl slid into the booth across from him. "But it looks like you could use some help." Billy thought for a minute, trying to figure out the best place to begin. Thankfully Darryl helped him out. "Why don't you start with why you're taking care of your brothers."

"Our mom died about a month after the twins were born." Billy hadn't told anyone this in a long time, and he started to relive some of the turmoil and pain. "She never recovered from the birth, and I came home from school and found her in bed. The boys were asleep next to her, and at first I thought she was sleeping, but she wouldn't wake up." He squeezed his eyes closed, willing his emotions to remain in check.

"You found your mom?"

"Yeah." He decided the only way he'd make it through this conversation was to keep going.

"It's still hard for you, isn't it?"

"Yeah, I miss her all the time." He released a soft sigh. "After her funeral, Dad wasn't the same. He tried to keep it together for all of us, but I had to step up and take care of the boys." He could see Darryl doing some quick math.

"That's a lot to ask of someone at sixteen."

"Maybe, but what was I going to do? They needed love, attention, and care. I learned very fast how to feed them, bathe them, change diapers, and rock them to sleep. They became the most important thing in the world to me. Dad worked second shift as a welder, so he'd watch them during the day, and I took care of them after school. After I graduated, I stayed at home because Dad couldn't handle the boys alone. By that time, he'd lost his job, and we moved wherever he could find another. About six months ago, we moved here."

"What happened to him?"

"He died two months ago. They said it was a heart attack, but I think it was a broken heart. He never got over losing my mom." Billy reached for a napkin and blew his nose. "He always said she was the love of his life." Billy sighed and felt tears threaten. He saw the sad look on Darryl's face and tried to discern if it was pity or something else. "After the funeral, there wasn't much money, and I couldn't afford the apartment any more. I managed to get the place we have, but I had to sell a lot of our stuff just to make the deposit." Billy swallowed hard and gave up, grief, fear, and months of anxiety catching up with him as tears began rolling down his cheeks. "We lived on cheap noodles and whatever I could get until the last of the money ran out." He felt the booth next to him shake, and then he was being hugged. That simple act of kindness stripped away the last of his self-control. It had been so long since he'd been held or hugged by anyone, he could barely remember it.

"It's okay. Just let it out," Darryl's soothing voice crooned softly in his ear.

"I tried to find work," Billy said against Darryl's chest, not wanting to do anything to make the man stop holding him. It just felt nice to have someone care for him, even if it was out of pity. "But no one was hiring, and I didn't have anyone to watch the boys." Billy sat up, and Darryl's arms fell away, leaving him with a light chill. "I stopped eating so I could make sure the boys had something to eat. And like a godsend, you agreed to hire me. I could hardly believe it, and then you fed me, but all the money I was making in tips went to get the rent up to date. I know I shouldn't have taken the food, but I had to feed the boys somehow." Billy felt miserable that he'd actually resorted to taking what amounted to garbage to feed his brothers. "Before what you gave them this afternoon, the boys hadn't eaten since last night." Billy felt tears start to well again but pushed them back with sheer willpower. "They cried this morning, they were so hungry."

"Who did the boys stay with?"

Billy wiped his eyes. "Our neighbor. She probably fed them a little, but she doesn't have much herself. The tip I got this afternoon will actually make the rest of this month's rent and give us a little for food. But God help us if one of the boys gets sick and has to go to the doctor." Billy felt one of his greatest fears shoot through him. Looking up, Billy expected to see pity, but what he saw was open-mouthed astonishment, and he didn't know what to make of it.

"We need to open for dinner in a few minutes, but I'll listen for the boys and make sure they have something to eat later, and afterward, we'll figure out how we can help."

"We?" Billy wasn't sure he'd heard him right. No one had helped him, in any way, in a very long time.

"Yeah. I'd like to try to help you if I can." Billy could hardly believe his ears and threw his arms around his boss in an exuberant display of relief. At first, Darryl seemed surprised, but then Billy felt the man's arms close around him, and he relaxed. For the first time since his dad died, there was light at the end of what had seemed to be a very long and very dark tunnel.

Darryl released him, and he grabbed a napkin, dabbing his eyes to get himself together. "Come on, let's check on the boys." Darryl flashed him a smile, and Billy wiped his eyes as he followed him to the office. Pushing the door open, he saw that both boys were still asleep, curled together.

Closing the door, Billy turned to his boss, not sure how he should thank the man for everything he'd done. He tried to form the words but just smiled instead, and Darryl returned it.

"Are you gonna kiss or what?" Billy jumped back as Sebastian teased from behind him. Thinking he was getting carried away, he followed the other server out front to make final preparations for dinner.

Billy made sure all the tables were set properly, letting his mind wander. Darryl had been so nice to him, and the man was handsome and he smelled really nice. Picking up more silverware and napkins, he set them on the last tables, wondering what it would be like to have those arms that had hugged him earlier pull him into another type of embrace, this one accompanied by the feel of Darryl's full lips against his. "Where are you, Billy?"

He jerked back and realized he'd put twice as many places at the table than he should have. "Sorry. I guess I was somewhere else for a minute."

"Thinking about Darryl, weren't you?" Sebastian asked as he bumped his shoulder.

"No!" he answered quickly, probably too quickly, and he felt himself blush.

"It's okay. I don't know much about his life, but I do know he's been alone for as long as I've worked here, and I think he's a little lonely."

"Do you think he—" Billy swallowed. "—likes boys?"

Sebastian began to giggle and covered his mouth with his hand, looking at the kitchen door. "I'm sure of it. From the way he looks at you, I'd say he interested in one boy in particular."

"No," Billy replied, feeling very self-conscious and embarrassed, turning away and looking around the room, anywhere but at Sebastian.

"Come on, Billy. I've seen it, and you must have too. Besides, I've seen the way you look and smile at him."

Billy turned and looked at Sebastian. "He's the one of the nicest men I've ever met." He thought of how Darryl had treated him, once he understood, and how the boys had taken to him, with even Donnie warming up to him. But mostly, he remembered the hug he'd received from the man. "It wouldn't be right to get involved with my boss. Besides, he's just being nice to me and the boys." Even as he said the words, he found he hoped they weren't true. He couldn't stop himself from looking at the door, almost as though if he stared at it hard enough, he'd develop X-ray vision and be able to see Darryl. Turning away, he said, "We should open the doors." Billy needed to change the subject so he could have a chance to think.

Sebastian nodded and walked to the front door, unlatching it, and Billy made one final pass through the dining room before they started what was bound to be a busy evening—and it was. Billy barely had time to think of anything but his customers, and yet every time he went into the kitchen, he saw Darryl smiling at him. It was weird in a nice sort of way. After his conversation with Sebastian, he couldn't help looking at his boss differently, and whenever he saw the man, he found himself smiling back.

"Biwwy." He looked over and saw Davey rubbing his eyes, standing outside Darryl's office. "I'm hungry." Billy saw Donnie follow his brother down the hall.

"Stay in the office, and I'll be right back." The boys went back inside, and Billy picked up his order and headed out to the dining room, placing the plates on the table. Turning around, he saw the kitchen door open and twin five-year-olds race through the dining room to where he stood, each grabbing a leg. They were followed almost immediately by Darryl, who scooped them both up, making airplane sounds as he carried them out of the dining room to peals of laughter and squeals of delight.

"Are they yours?" the older lady at the table asked with a smile on her face.

"They're my brothers," Billy replied, watching as the door swung closed behind them. He couldn't help marveling at how happy Darryl seemed to make the boys. They'd laughed today, something neither of them had done much of since their father's death.

"Well, they're just precious," the lady replied as she tasted her mussels, then put down her fork. "These are marvelous, but I was wondering. When I read the menu, I noticed that you were offering eels, and I was wondering what they were like." She peered up at him sheepishly.

"I'll see if the chef can arrange for a taste." He nodded to the lady and the man with her before leaving their table. Heading to the kitchen, he opened the door and was shocked to see the boys, each with aprons wrapped around them, standing at a makeshift table near the salad station.

"We're helping," they said in unison before returning to putting bread in the baskets. Billy couldn't contain his laughter when he saw their little hands swimming inside disposable plastic gloves. Billy looked to Darryl, who just shrugged, and at Julio, who was doing his best to keep from laughing his ass off. Both boys were happy as anything, even if Darryl's usually precise breadbaskets looked like they'd been put together by five-year-olds... wait, they were!

"Could I get a tasting of the eels for a customer?" Billy asked Darryl through his smile, stepping closer. "You're great with the boys. I haven't seen them this happy in months." Billy turned away again, suddenly filled with the feeling that he wasn't doing enough for his brothers. He couldn't even feed them properly and was having trouble keeping a roof over their heads.

"They adore you, Billy." It almost seemed as though Darryl was reading his mind. "And you've done a great job with them. Don't ever think otherwise." Darryl put a small portion of the eels on the pickup counter.

"Biwwy, look what we did." Davey held up a basket so full of stacked bread, it was doing an imitation of the leaning tower of Pisa.

"I'll take this out." Billy smirked at his boss. "You better supervise your help." He hoped he wasn't out of line, and Darryl just grinned back at him.

"I guess so." Darryl walked over to the boys as Billy picked up the plate and took it out front, placing it in front of the customer with a small flourish. The dinner rush was winding down, and the restaurant became quieter, with a number of customers talking at the bar and a few stragglers enjoying drinks and dessert.

"I love this time in the evening." Sebastian came up behind him. "Everyone's happy and enjoying themselves. It's sort of like the afterglow." Sebastian winked at him, and Billy snickered before going to work cleaning up the tables.

Between the remaining customers and getting things ready for the next day, the servers and bussers were busy for the rest of the evening. Whenever Billy was in the kitchen, the boys seemed happy, and an hour before closing, he'd found them again in Darryl's office, eating hot dogs and frites, sitting on what looked like an old tablecloth on the floor. The next time he checked, they were again asleep on the futon, curled up together under Darryl's throw.

"They're incredible," Darryl said softly from behind him.

"I can't thank you enough for what you've done for them." Billy felt his throat start to close as his emotions took over. "This is way beyond what any boss should have to do." He was still convinced Darryl was just being an above-and-beyond boss. Billy felt a hand on his shoulder.

"I didn't do it because I'm your boss. I did it because you needed help, and because—" Darryl cut himself off, and Billy turned around, looking into his eyes, wondering what he wanted to say. He almost let it go, but he just couldn't. "Because...?" he prompted. Billy watched Darryl for a while, multiple emotions flickering quickly across the man's face, but the one he saw most strongly was doubt and confusion.

"Because I like you. But you work for me, and I shouldn't, not like I do." Darryl backed away slowly, and Billy reached out, touching his hand lightly. Darryl stopped, and Billy tightened his grip, letting his fingers ghost over the skin of Darryl's arm. Touching this man felt like he was touching a live wire, and he didn't want to let go.

Davey stirred and wiped his eyes, yawning before settling again. Billy felt Darryl's hand slip from his, and he bent down and straightened his brother's blanket. When he turned back toward the door, it was empty. Billy knew he shouldn't feel let down, but he did somehow, like he was missing something. But how could you miss what you never had?

Leaving the office, Billy walked through the kitchen and noticed that Darryl barely looked up at him as he passed, but it only took a glance to see the conflict on the man's face, and it was also obvious that he was trying to hide it. Billy stopped to ask him about it but turned and went through the doors to the dining room instead and got right back to work, barely thinking about what he was doing, his mind on what Darryl had said. "I like you." *He said that he liked me.*

"What's with you?" Sebastian whispered from behind the bar as he filled a beer glass.

Billy came out of his own thoughts. "Nothing." Sebastian left to deliver the beer and then returned, standing near him as they watched the customers to make sure they didn't need anything, but Billy's gaze kept moving to the kitchen door.

"Let's get this place finished so we can go home." Sebastian bumped his shoulder, and they shared a smile before seeing to their customers and getting the dining room ready for the morning.

At closing time, Sebastian locked the front door. The last of the cleanup had been finished, and Billy headed to the back room. Passing through the kitchen, he didn't see Darryl until he got to the office door. He was inside, sitting in his chair, watching the boys sleep, a dazed sort of look on his face. Billy coughed slightly, and Darryl lifted his head, his eyes definitely a little puffy. "Everything's closed and cleaned up. I'm going to take the boys home." He kept his voice low and soft.

"I'll help you." Darryl got up and turned away. Billy thought he might have wiped his eyes. Then he walked to the futon and gently picked up Davey, who wrapped his little arms around Darryl's neck and rested his head against his shoulder. Billy picked up Donnie and the twin did the same thing to him, neither of them really waking up.

"I got things here, guys. I'll see you in the morning," Julio said as he continued cleaning up. Darryl stopped a second, probably to argue, but Julio seemed to have his number.

"Thanks," Darryl replied, and he walked out the back door, leading them to his car. Somehow the man managed to unlock the door with his arms full of five-year-old little boy, and he settled him on the seat. Davey made small noises, and as Billy put Donnie on the seat, the two of them leaned against one another, their big eyes closing again as the doors closed.

Billy slid into the passenger seat and waited for Darryl, who still hadn't said anything more to him. Quite frankly, it was starting to make him feel uncomfortable. Looking over at the driver's side door, he watched as Darryl slid down into the supple leather of the driver's seat. Before starting the car, Darryl looked over at him and swallowed hard. Then he rested his head against the steering wheel and let out what must have been the most agonized sigh in the history of man. Billy had no idea what to say, since he didn't know what was bothering Darryl, but he reached over and stroked his hand down the older man's back. At the first touch, Darryl raised his head slowly. "You must think I'm some kind of freak."

Billy shook his head no and looked deep into Darryl's agonized eyes. "I think you're the sweetest, kindest man I've ever met, and I like you too." Billy waited, hoping Darryl would say something, but he just started the car and pulled out of the spot, leaving Billy feeling like a complete fool.

It was a short drive to the Molly, and Darryl parked the car out front. They each carried one of the boys up the stairs to the apartment. "I've got them from here," Billy said harshly. He knew he was being cool to his boss, but he'd actually come as close as he'd ever come to telling someone that he cared for them, and Darryl had blown him off. Billy unlocked the door and walked inside the dinky apartment. "I'll get them ready for bed. You don't have to stay—you probably have things to do, anyway."

Billy turned on one of the lights in the corner and carried Donnie inside. The twin boys were awake now, and Darryl set Davey on his feet. "Both of you go into the bathroom and brush your teeth."

"Do we have to, Biwwy? We're not sleepy," Donnie replied as he yawned.

"Go on and I'll read you a story once you're in bed." Billy watched the boys go into the bathroom. Billy then noticed that Darryl was waiting in the doorway, chewing nervously on a finger nail. "Thank you for everything you did today. It was very nice of you." God, he sounded so formal, but Darryl had him so confused.

"I like you, Billy, I really do." Darryl took a step closer. "But you're so young, and…." Darryl took another step, and Billy let himself hope.

"I'm an adult, Darryl, and I know my own mind." He looked into the bathroom and saw the boys standing on the stepstool brushing their teeth. Billy turned back to Darryl and saw the man stop, looking confused again.

"I wish I did," Darryl replied. "Maybe I should go."

Billy stepped closer. "What is it you're afraid of?"

Darryl just watched him before shaking his head slowly. "I can't talk about it." Darryl took a small step back. Billy could see the suppressed pain and fear suddenly burst onto Darryl's face. What could reduce the confident man he worked for to a nervous wreck?

"Okay, but if you want to, I'll listen." Billy stepped closer to Darryl. "Thank you for everything." He looked up at Darryl, seeing him lick his lips, and Billy let his eyes drift closed. But nothing happened. Opening his eyes again, he saw that Darryl hadn't moved. Leaning forward slowly, he waited for Darryl to pull away, but he didn't. Billy moved closer and felt his lips touch Darryl's. A small zing went through him, and he felt Darryl's lips respond and then felt hands slide along his cheeks, holding him softly as the kiss deepened.

"Ooooh." Billy heard the boys behind him. Smiling into the kiss, he pulled away and smiled at Darryl, wanting very much to do that again. "Biwwy's kissing," the boys crooned together, and thankfully Darryl smiled as well.

Darryl was the first to speak. "I should go." Darryl leaned close and gave him another kiss before walking down the hall to the stairs.

Billy closed the door. "Come on, boys, let's get you into bed." Billy helped the boys get undressed, into their pajamas, and settled in their bed. Sitting on the edge of the bed, he reached over to the small shelf and pulled down a very worn copy of *Babar* and began to read. The boys were asleep by the time he finished, and Billy turned off the light and got ready for bed himself, tasting Darryl's lips as he climbed beneath the covers.

CHAPTER FIVE

DARRYL practically floated down the stairs of Billy's building in a daze. He'd felt that soft kiss all the way to his toes, and damn if Billy hadn't tasted like heaven. His entire body tingled, and he was so excited that he could barely contain himself. The euphoric feeling lasted until he got into his car, and then the worries and doubts began to play in his head in that same scolding voice that always chastised him whenever he had these feelings. He hated that voice, but he couldn't seem to stop it.

He knew he was going to see Billy almost every day and that avoiding him was impossible, especially after that tender kiss. He'd tried to cut himself off from what he'd been feeling, but his young server and his two brothers had gotten under his skin so fast, he hadn't had time to stop them. Walking up the front walk, he fished out his keys and his phone. Unlocking the door, he set his keys on the entry table and began dialing. "Mom, it's Darryl."

"Hi, dear, you just getting home?"

He heard her pleasant voice and felt the knot inside loosen a little. "Yeah."

"You don't sound very good. Are you okay?" Her voice went from happy to concerned in a second.

"No. I've got something I need to ask you about, and I don't know how to do it." Darryl sank into his leather chair in front of the blank television set. "I know we don't talk about this anymore, but I need to."

"You know you can talk to me about anything." Even as she said the right thing, her voice sounded wary.

"Even Connor?" Darryl whispered, and the line went silent for a long time.

"Yes, even Connor." He could almost see his mom slowly lowering herself into one of the kitchen chairs. "I'd hoped that things like that were behind you."

"Things like what? Falling in love?" A tear rolled down Darryl's cheek, and he brushed it away. This wasn't the time to get emotional, it was the time to talk things through, and he knew if he began to cry she'd hear him and would start in too.

"No, dear." Her voice was very clear and almost authoritative. "We want you to fall in love." She sniffed softly. "I'd always hoped I'd have grandchildren, and I accept that's not going to happen, but I want you to fall in love and be happy. I worry that you're alone so much."

"I may have met someone, but he's...." Damn, all the old guilt and self-recrimination came flooding back. He just couldn't go through all that pain again.

"How young is he?" She sounded as though she was bracing herself for the worst shock of her life.

"Billy's twenty-one."

"He's...." His mother's voice flooded with relief, and then the concern floated back in. "I don't understand the problem, dear, or what this has to do with the Connor incident.... Shit!" she swore vehemently. "I knew it. I knew that quack was fucking wrong."

"Mom!" He reacted to her cursing; she never swore. Then the rest of what she'd said sank in. "Quack?"

"I'm so sorry, dear." He could hear her start to cry on the other end of the phone. "I knew what they said couldn't be true, but we were so scared for you and did what they wanted." He heard her sniff and then blow her nose. "I wish I could be there to talk this through with you in person, but suffice it to say that everything Dr. Holcomb told you was probably a sack of shit. The thought that I let that man anywhere near my little boy breaks my heart."

"You mean I'm not...." Darryl couldn't bring himself to say the word. He'd had it leveled at him so many times years ago that it caught in his throat.

"I doubt it. If I get my hands on him, I'll wring the old fart's neck."

"So there's nothing wrong with me now?" Darryl could hardly believe his ears. He'd longed for someone to believe him for so long, and they had, sort of, they just hadn't said anything.

"I don't think there ever was." Now he heard her sobbing. "To think of the hell we let them put you through." Her tears brought his own. While hers were regret, his were unadulterated relief, and he felt a sense of hope start to rise within him as a part of himself that he'd kept closed off for so long began to open up. "You don't have feelings for...."

"No," Darryl said with a smile. "I never have, Mom. I just fell in love with Connor. Hell, I was still in high school." He could barely keep himself from jumping around the living room.

"I know, dear, and your father and I both regret the way we reacted." She sniffed again. "We both love you and hope you can forgive us."

Darryl heard what sounded like another phone pick up. "I just wanted you to hear it from me as well." His father's booming voice rang through the line.

"Why did you wait so long? I've been carrying this around with me forever."

"We thought it was over, and you never talked about it, so we didn't either." He could hear the regret in his dad's voice. "I wish your mother and I could have had this conversation with you face to face, but I'm glad we're having it nonetheless."

"All this time I thought there was something wrong with me." The words came out almost as a plea.

"We realize that now." His father's usually steady voice sounded harsh, like he was fighting back tears himself. "As your mother said, we hope you can forgive us."

Darryl sighed and settled back in the chair. "Of course I do." What else could he say? "You were only doing your best."

"Will you come for a visit soon?" his mom asked hopefully.

"I was about to ask you the same thing. I'd love for you to see my restaurant." He let his renewed excitement carry away the hurt from earlier. It was over, and he wasn't going to dwell on it.

"We'll do that soon," his mom said, catching a bit of Darryl's excitement. "It's getting late, and I know you get up early. We love you, and we'll talk soon."

Darryl heard another sniffle as he said goodbye and closed the phone. Without getting out of his chair, he looked around his room with fresh eyes. Everything seemed brighter, cleaner, like it was all fresh and new. Lifting himself out of the chair, he went to his bedroom and got cleaned up before going to bed, dreaming the dreams of the happy.

In the morning, Darryl cleaned up quickly, but instead of going downstairs for his morning ritual, he made a detour up to the attic. Turning on the light, he began rummaging through the boxes. "I know I put that stuff she sent...." Darryl rummaged further back. "Aha!" he said to himself as he found the box he wanted, pulling it out and taking it back downstairs, setting it in the hall. Pouring himself a cup of coffee, he drank it standing at the sink before washing the cup and grabbing his jacket. Picking up the box, he walked outside.

The morning was bright and clear, with a spring crispness in the air. Making his decision, he decided to walk and started toward the corner. Everything seemed just a little... more—the blossoms smelled sweeter, the sky was just a little bluer, and he felt lighter both inside and out. Even the Molly didn't seem quite as rundown as he approached the front door. He debated going in and seeing Billy and almost went inside, but he decided the man deserved his privacy.

"What the hell." Changing his mind, Darryl turned around, going inside and taking the stairs to Billy's floor, knocking softly. The door opened slowly, and he saw Billy's bright eyes through the crack and the door opened farther. "I thought I'd stop by and see if I could take you to breakfast. I know the chef at the restaurant down the street, and he makes a mean omelet." Darryl smiled and leaned in for a kiss, but Billy pulled back, looking at him warily.

"Last night you said you liked me, but would barely touch me, and now you're all happy and lovey-dovey. I don't get it." Billy's eyes narrowed, his jaw set.

"I know, and I'm sorry for that. I found out some things from my mom last night, and it helped put a number of things in focus. I'd like to tell you about it this afternoon." Billy's eyes widened, but he didn't say anything. "You said you'd listen, and I think it's time I told someone. You told me about yourself, so I thought I should do the same." Darryl handed Billy the box. "My mom gave me a number of my old things a while ago, and it included this box of old toys. I thought the boys might like them."

"Come inside. I'm just getting the boys dressed." Billy stepped back, and Darryl went into the apartment. The boys were standing on their bed, bouncing up and down.

"Dawwyl," Davey called as he jumped off the bed and launched himself into Darryl's arms, laughing as he was caught and flown around the room. "What's dat?" He pointed to the box, and Darryl put him down, both boys peering at the box Billy was carrying.

"Darryl brought you some things." Billy closed the door and set the box down, the boys peering over the rim, gasping as they reached inside. "You need to say thank you."

Two sets of eyes looked at him. "Fank you," they both crooned before pulling everything out of the box, strewing all the toys on the floor. Then Donnie climbed into the box and closed the lid. Darryl laughed as Davey began running one of the cars around the room.

"We need to get you dressed," Billy said as he lifted the lid on the box.

"Do we have to go to the lady's?" Donnie asked as Billy picked him up.

"Yeah, she smells," Davey added, scrunching his face.

"Not today. Darryl's taking us to breakfast, and then I have to go to work."

"Are we going to work too?" Davey asked as his car skittered across the floor.

"Actually, I thought if you were good, you could play with your new toys in my office," Darryl said to two pairs of eyes. "But you need to get dressed for Billy so we can get going."

Both boys stopped what they were doing and raced to the bathroom, with Billy following behind. Darryl picked up the toys as he heard Billy and the boys in the bathroom. Obviously, getting them dressed was quite an ordeal. As he was picking up the last of the toys, the bathroom door flew open, and Davey ran out in his underwear, grabbing the car from under the table and running back into the bathroom.

It took awhile, but Billy finally got the boys dressed and ready to go. Darryl held Davey's hand and carried the box as they made it down the stairs and out onto the sidewalk.

They entered the restaurant through the back, Maureen looking up from her work with a smile. "Morning, Maureen," Darryl called. "These are Billy's brothers, Davey and Donnie." The boys hid behind Billy's legs, peeking around until Maureen approached holding a cookie in each hand. Shyness flew right out the window and their little hands reached forward, taking the cookies, and the boys jabbered their thank-yous before stuffing them in their mouths.

Darryl put the box of toys on the floor in his office and began changing his shirt. He heard Billy outside, talking softly to the twins.

"You need to stay in the office unless Darryl asks you to do something for him. You can play with your toys, and I'll be in on my breaks to read to you." He wished he could see their little faces, but Darryl imagined them nodding vigorously. "Darryl will bring you something to eat soon, and I have to get to work. Will you promise to be good?"

"Yes, Biwwy," they crooned in unison, and then the two little ones burst into the office and raced for the box of toys, digging into it again.

"Are you sure this is okay?" Billy asked him from the doorway, watching the boys run trucks along the floor.

"Of course. There's nothing in here that they can hurt unless they really try, and it should be safe for them. I removed anything harmful yesterday." Darryl chuckled as Davey began running his trucks up the walls. "You should really keep them on the floor."

Davey stopped and big eyes looked him over, and he moved to the floor, running the truck beneath the futon and under the small table. Billy gave each boy a hug and a kiss before leaving the office and walking through to the dining room. Darryl left right behind him, leaving the door open. He'd no sooner left the room when a truck came racing behind him, barreling into the wall across the small hallway, a rushing Donnie behind it.

"Why don't you get a couple milk crates and place them in the doorway?" Maureen called with a chuckle in her voice. "It'll stop any runaways." Darryl did as she suggested and went into his kitchen and started breakfast.

"What's with the kids?" Maureen asked as she continued icing a cake for a party they had booked for that evening. Darryl told her about the previous day's developments, and as he did, her mouth hung open further and further. "I don't know which I find more amazing, Billy taking care of his brothers, or you finally admitting that you like someone."

"I'm not that bad," Darryl scoffed as he cracked eggs into a bowl.

Maureen threw a bit of icing, hitting Darryl on the cheek. "You bloody well are, and you know it." She continued frosting her cake, and Darryl wiped away the icing with a smile. "I just could never figure out why." Darryl saw her stop working as she turned to him. "I always thought someone must have really hurt you pretty badly."

Darryl put some ham and onion on the grill, letting them warm before pouring the egg mixture over the top. He toasted some bread as well. "They did, but not in the way you'd expect." He found to his surprise that it didn't hurt to talk about it the way it always had before. Things had changed, and Darryl could have jumped for joy because of it.

"You gonna tell me about it?" She finished what she was doing and placed the cake in the cooler before cleaning up after herself.

"I think so." He finished what he was doing, not looking up from the grill, his old apprehension returning.

"You know that whatever it is won't make a difference." Maureen swatted his behind with a towel. "I'll still love ya." She swatted him again before returning to work.

Darryl finished making the breakfast and found Billy in the dining room, folding napkins. He looked up and smiled as he worked, making Darryl's insides clench. That smile just got him right in his heart every time. Knowing the man was just as sweet as his smile really got him going. "Breakfast is ready."

Billy set his work aside, and Darryl held the door for him. Grabbing the plates, they carried them back to the office. The boys gathered around, and Billy got them settled. They gingerly tasted the eggs before deeming them okay and tucking in.

Darryl forked his eggs, but he wasn't very hungry. "When I was in high school, I had a friend named Connor. We met when he was in ninth grade. I was a year ahead of him, but he was so smart that we ended up in a lot of the same classes, and we became friends." Darryl watched as Billy ate slowly, his attention on him. "To make a long story short, a few years later, we both found out that we liked the football players a lot more than we cared for the cheerleaders."

Billy swallowed and nodded gently. "I understand what that feels like."

He felt Billy's finger gently stroke the back of his hand and then stop.

Darryl set down his fork and took Billy's hand in his. "Over time, our friendship led to something more. We used to stay over at each other's house sometimes, and…." Darryl swallowed, not sure he wanted to share what he and Connor had with anyone, not even Billy. The memories were too precious to him. "You get the picture."

Billy set down his fork, his eyes glued to Darryl's. "I take it things didn't end well."

"No, they didn't. Connor's dad found us together in his room. We'd thought they'd gone to bed, and Connor and I were"—Darryl swallowed hard—"in the middle of things." He could still see the hurt look on Connor's face. It wasn't that his dad had caught him, but the names the man had hurled at his son still made Darryl cringe. "His dad pulled him off the bed and began hitting him. I tried to shield him, but the man just pulled me away and continued beating Connor, calling him the worst names possible." Darryl felt the suppressed emotions come surging to the surface. "I haven't told anyone about this, ever." Darryl looked at the boys, who had finished eating and returned to their toys.

"Finally he wore down and stormed around the room, throwing my clothes at me. I managed to dress, and he shoved me out the door." Darryl swallowed hard. "The last thing I saw was Connor trying to hide beneath his covers."

"What did you do?"

"I ran home like a big fat coward. My mom and dad were up, and Connor's dad had already called."

"That must have been hard." Billy stroked his hand again.

Darryl laughed through his hurt. "That was the easy part. My mom cried, and my dad looked like he'd been shot or something, but they sent me to bed and said we'd discuss it in the morning. I didn't sleep a wink that night, worrying about Connor and my mom and dad."

"What did they do?"

"At first, nothing. They tried to understand and talked to me about what I was feeling. It amazed me that they still loved me and everything. I thought they might have reacted the way Connor's dad had, but they didn't. They did their best to understand."

"I don't understand what the problem was," Billy added, looking confused.

"The problem started the next afternoon when Connor's dad came over. He was some minister at one of those churches that think gay people can be cured. I had just turned eighteen, and Connor was still underage, so it was either enter their program or go to jail as a sex offender." Darryl covered his eyes and tried not to think of what could have happened. "Sometimes I think that would have been preferable. I spent a month away from home in their program, and then I saw this psychologist who told me for months that I was some sort of pedophile and that I had to suppress my urge to be with little boys."

Billy's eyes widened, and Darryl saw him look at the boys, both of them still happily playing.

"I'm not. I have no interest in boys, never have." Darryl felt the tears well in his eyes. "But I suppose after hearing something again and again and again, you start to wonder. I was only a kid, and a doctor kept telling me I was sick, that I liked boys and I had to fight it. They punished me every time I got excited by pictures of men, which they kept showing me just so they could punish me. After awhile, I did my best to go along with them just to get away."

Billy tightened his grip on Darryl's hand. "Let me guess, you started to believe it?"

Darryl nodded once. "I haven't allowed myself much company over the last ten years or so. Oh, I dated a little and went out, but mostly just for impersonal sex. I've always been afraid—they made me afraid. The first time I tried to have sex after Connor, all I could see was his dad hitting him. I actually had to leave and be sick."

"You must have carried this with you for years. What changed?" Billy asked. He *ooof*ed as Donnie landed on his lap.

"I told my mom about you, and we talked about it. I guess she told me that they were wrong to ever let any of those religious wackos near me and that they loved and believed in me. I guess I finally saw through all the crap that I'd been sort of programmed with. I realized what I'd been missing and that I owed you an explanation—and a confession."

Darryl sat back as Davey climbed onto his lap, arms wrapping around his neck. "You need a hug," Davey said, squeezing him around the neck before climbing back down and going back to running his truck around the floor.

"What sort of confession?" Darryl could hear something strange in Billy's voice, but he couldn't quite figure out what it was.

"I didn't lie to you last night, I like you. Hell, I really like you." Darryl reached out, stroking a hand along Billy's cheek. "I can't say I'm not scared, but I'd like to"—he wasn't sure how to do this—"ask you on a date." There, he'd said it. Something he hadn't done since he'd asked Connor on their first date all those years ago.

"I'd love to. But we may have some chaperones to deal with." Billy smiled as Donnie skidded off his lap and began playing on the floor with his brother.

"The restaurant is closed on Sundays. I thought you and the boys could come over for the day. Maybe we could go to the park for the afternoon."

"Why?" Billy whispered, his voice barely audible. "I'm just some kid who can barely feed himself and his brothers. Why would you want to date me? Is it because you feel sorry for us?"

"No!" Darryl replied loudly, then softened his voice. "It's because you're caring and one of the sweetest men I've ever met. And you make my heart feel light and alive for the first time I can remember since Connor."

"What happened to him?"

"The last time I saw him, he was bruised and could barely see. Before I got out of the program, his family had moved away, and I never found out where. I've always hoped he found a way to be happy somehow." Darryl looked into Billy's eyes, waiting for his answer.

"Yes, I'll go on a date with you." The back door opened and closed, pulling their attention away from each other. "But I need to get to work before my boss decides I'm slacking." Billy winked and stood up. "You two be good. Darryl and I have to get to work now." Both boys looked up, nodding their heads before returning to their toys.

Darryl stacked the dishes to take to the dish room while Billy made sure the boys were okay. Leaving the room, they returned the milk crates to their place in the doorway. After dropping off the dishes, Darryl got to work. He couldn't help feeling like he'd just won the lottery.

CHAPTER SIX

BILLY had barely slept at all. Their tiny apartment was quiet, and he could hear the occasional sound of one of the boys moving in their bed. Staring at the stained ceiling, he let his mind run over the past week and the change it had brought to their lives. Looking across the dim room, he could see Davey holding a stuffed bear under his arm, while Donnie rested next to a purple hippopotamus. Both had been gifts from Sebastian. It seemed everyone in the restaurant had tried to help them in one way or another. Maureen had brought in a huge box of clothes that her son had outgrown. They were still a little big, but at least they wouldn't have to worry about things to wear next winter.

And the toys—it seemed as though everyone at the restaurant had brought something in for the boys. They had trucks and the stuffed animals they were now sleeping with on a nightly basis. Maureen had brought in some building blocks, and Davey had fought his brother whenever Donnie got near them. Donnie got even by claiming the set of barnyard animals that Mary Ellen, one of the other part-time servers, had brought in for them. Billy smiled in his bed as he thought of how everyone had sort of adopted and watched over his brothers. Other than his family, Billy had never felt as though he fit in anywhere, but Café Belgie was starting to feel like a home to him, with Darryl at its heart.

"Biwwy," he heard a small voice call though the darkness.

Pushing back the covers, he got out of bed and carefully walked across the room. "What is it, Donnie?"

The little boy sat up, wiping his eyes. "Davey keeps kicking me." He glared down at his sleeping brother. "Can I sweep with you?"

"Sure." Billy lifted his brother, the covers falling away. Donnie reached for his hippo. "Herbie needs to stay here."

Donnie gave him a look for a second and then hugged him around the neck, and Billy carried him to the bed. "Are we going to visit Dawwyl today?" Donnie settled under the covers, yawning as Billy got back into bed.

"Yes. He'll be here when it gets light out. Now go to sleep." The youngster rolled over and promptly did as he was told, with Billy following behind him.

When Billy woke hours later, it wasn't to the spring sunshine drifting through the windows or the relaxing sound of birds singing, but to the noise of car crashes and the little boy sound of gunning truck engines. "Vroom, vroom, brrrrake, crash." Checking the small clock by his bed, he saw it was six-thirty. Good God! He thought about telling the boys to be quiet but knew that was a lost cause. Once they got going, they were a bundle of energy. Not that he was going to complain. Over the past week they'd started acting more like healthy five-year-olds. "Will you play with us?" Davey asked as he crashed his truck into Donnie's.

"Actually, we need to get both of you bathed and dressed so we can be ready when Darryl comes." Billy lifted the little boy off the floor, and he made a last minute grab for his truck. "You don't want to take that in the tub with you, it'll rust." Davey looked at Billy as if he were nuts and clutched his truck as they made for the bathroom. While the tub filled, Billy rounded up Donnie and got both boys in the water without their toys. Not that they needed them. The small apartment bathroom was soon filled with boyish squeals as they splashed each other and Billy. "That's enough. Let's get you washed and dry so we can eat." Food always got them moving, and soon Billy was wrapping each of them in the only towels he had.

Davey squirmed out of his and raced through the apartment naked, his little legs and butt going as he pulled open a drawer and began pulling on his underpants. "I can do it! See!" he yelled proudly as he tried to put on his shirt inside-out. Billy laughed and carried Donnie airplane-style to the dresser and pulled out his clothes for him. Donnie got dressed while Billy helped Davey fix his clothes. With both boys finally ready, with even their shoes on, Billy was finally able to dress himself, and just in time, because he heard a soft knock on the door. Cracking it open, he saw Darryl standing in the hallway.

"Morning," Darryl said as he leaned close, and Billy smiled as he was given a soft kiss. "I thought we could go back to my house for breakfast and then to the park."

"That'd be nice." He wasn't quite sure about dating yet, but it was definitely nice to have someone paying attention to him. Billy nearly jumped when he felt Darryl's hand on his back, stroking lightly.

"Can we take our stuff with us?" Davey asked from the floor as he played with his truck.

"I have something for you at my house," Darryl replied, "but you have to put your toys away here first." Little feet flew around the room, putting the scattered toys in the box before bounding into Darryl's arms with squeals that they were ready. "Are you ready?" Darryl asked Billy.

Darryl looked at him, his eyes smoldering, and Billy's mouth went dry. "I'm ready." They left the apartment and walked down the stairs, each of the twins holding one of Darryl's hands. They walked to the corner and then down the block. Billy kept looking around, wondering where Darryl was leading them, until they stopped in front of a white row house with black shutters and colorful window boxes planted with spring flowers.

Darryl unlocked the door as Davey pulled on Billy's pant leg. "I gotta go potty," the little boy stage-whispered, and he began clutching himself, bouncing from leg to leg.

Billy held his hand, and as soon as the door was open, Darryl lifted Davey and they stepped inside. Darryl whisked Davey away, footsteps echoing through the house, as Billy and Donnie stood in the small entrance hall. "Wow," Billy muttered under his breath as he peeked into the living room. High ceilings, tall windows, and gleaming honey floors greeted him, along with large pieces of comfortable-looking leather furniture. It wasn't fussy but clean and comfortable with touches of elegance, particularly in the fireplace and the old crystal chandelier. Billy didn't want to snoop, but he couldn't help it, and he moved to the end of the hall, peering into the dining room with its large, elegant table and chairs, glimmering lights fixtures, and deep-red walls. "Do you like it?" Darryl's voice whispered in his ear, warm breath flowing across the skin of his neck.

"Your home is beautiful." Billy turned around and found Darryl so close he could feel the heat from his body.

"So are you." Darryl's eyes blazed.

Billy prepared to be kissed, but a chorus of "I'm hungry" from the little peanut gallery interrupted them, so Darryl led him through to the surprisingly tiny kitchen. "I loved the house when I saw it and almost didn't buy it because of the kitchen, but I do most of my cooking at the restaurant anyway, so...," Darryl explained as he started what Billy figured was the beginning of French toast.

"It's still really nice." He ran his hand over the cool granite countertops. It might not be very large, but it was a lot nicer than his old battered sink, stove, and refrigerator in what was probably once a closet. "Is there anything we can do to help?" Billy noticed that the boys were already starting to explore the house.

"I've got the cooking under control. If you'd like"—he pointed to a door off the kitchen—"you can take the boys into the backyard."

Turning around, Billy saw Davey disappear around the corner. Hurrying to catch up, he caught the youngster in another small hallway and heard Donnie already laughing with delight. Holding Davey's hand, he followed the sounds into a bedroom, where Donnie was already jumping on the bed. "Get down." Donnie stopped bouncing, knowing he'd done something wrong. Turning around, he slid off the mattress, and Billy straightened the blankets before taking each boy by the hand and leading them through the house to the kitchen. Opening the door, they walked out into a small, paved yard lined with blooming plants. As soon as Billy let go of the boys' hands, they raced to the corner, peering into the tiny pond, running their hands through the fountain.

"There's fish!" Donnie exclaimed, pointing and staring at the large orange and yellow fish as they glided through the water. Donnie knelt down and nearly took a header into the pond. The only thing that stopped it was Billy grabbing the waistband of his pants.

"They can't hurt anything out here," Darryl said from the doorway.

"Except maybe traumatize your fish," Billy retorted before cautioning the boys not to get into the water. They seemed to lose some of their interest and wandered off to explore the rest of the yard.

"Breakfast will be ready in a few minutes. Would you help me with the plates?" Darryl asked, and after another check on the boys, Billy went inside.

"Your yard is beautiful. Are you sure the boys won't hurt anything?"

"Everything out there is pretty hardy." Darryl showed him where the plates were and started dishing up the food. "I thought we'd eat outside. The sun should be warming the yard, and it's a wonderful day." The kitchen was small enough that Darryl just leaned over and touched his lips to Billy's. A few seconds later, Billy heard Darryl set the food on the counter and big arms were wrapped around him, pulling him closer as Darryl's lips and tongue devoured his mouth. The small room filled with tiny moans and whimpers that Billy realized were his. Darryl's hands slid down his back, and he started but didn't pull back when they cupped his butt before pressing them closer together.

"Should we...," he started to ask, but he gave up as his lips were taken again, this time with more force and desire. Whatever he was going to say was lost in the taste of Darryl's lips and the heat of his body pressed against him. He could feel Darryl's excitement against his hip, sliding against his own jeans-encased erection. "If you don't stop, I'm gonna come," Billy whispered before Darryl lightened the kiss and slowly backed away.

"I want to see that more than anything." Darryl's eyes shone, and Billy half expected him to continue, but shouts from outside pulled them apart. "Why don't you see to the wrecking crew outside, and I'll join you in a minute." Darryl winked at him and smiled. Billy grabbed the plates and went outside.

"Davey, don't climb the fence," Billy admonished, and his brother stepped back onto solid ground as Donnie stood peering between the slats, trying to stick his hand through.

"My truck," he whined softly, continuing to try to reach through. Where had they gotten those? Billy wondered silently until he saw a few others scattered around. Darryl must have been prepared.

"We'll get it after we eat." Billy tugged him away from the fence, and he continued whining but sat in a chair as Billy distributed the plates and forks. "Darryl made French toast." Both boys looked at him, tilting their heads slightly.

"I've got food for the bottomless pits." Darryl set down the tray and tickled the boys lightly before setting down their plates. Both boys stared at the food, looking at each other and Billy but not eating a bite. "What's wrong?"

"I don't think they know what it is. Dad never made things like this. Mostly we had cereal, maybe eggs occasionally, but nothing this elaborate." Billy sat down, suddenly feeling like he and his dad had been depriving the boys all this time. "Try it guys, it's good," Billy encouraged as he took a bite, closing his eyes as cinnamon and butter burst onto his tongue.

The boys got the idea and began to eat, grinning after their first bite and digging in with gusto. Once they started, they always seemed to eat in such a huge hurry, like someone was going to take their food away. Billy knew it was because they'd gone hungry.

"What is it? You look so sadly distracted," Darryl asked, his hand stroking over Billy's.

"Sometimes I feel like such a failure." Billy set down his fork. "I can't even feed them without help and can barely afford the dingy rooms we live in. They deserve better than that."

"What they deserve is someone who loves them more than anything else in the world," Darryl whispered softly, and Billy looked over at his brothers, both of them stuffing their faces and grinning, bits of French toast on their teeth. "See, they're happy. You know that they don't need a bunch of things or a fancy house— they just need to be loved."

"But I can't even feed them without help." His desperation and fear that the struggle just for food would return when Darryl's generosity dried up wrenched his gut.

"There's nothing wrong with accepting help when you need it." Billy turned toward Darryl and felt a rough palm slide over his cheek. "I haven't felt needed by anyone in a long time. It's nice to know that I can help them"—Billy saw Darryl swallow—"and you." Billy watched as Darryl ate a bite of his breakfast, but his eyes never left him, and Billy found that he liked being the center of this man's attention. It felt good, like he was cared for.

Something inside wasn't ready to let it go. "But what if you're not here?"

Something flashed in Darryl's eyes that Billy didn't recognize. "I'm not planning on going anywhere in a hurry, so just relax a little. The boys are happy, and I hope you are too."

Billy nodded a little. He was happy. Darryl seemed to make both him and the boys happy. Hell, the man had made him breakfast on his day off and brought them back to his home… and endangered his fish. "I know you're right."

"So don't worry about it. Just relax and have a little fun." Darryl finished eating and sat back. "You boys done eating?" Both boys grinned and nodded their heads. The twins' plates were clean, and they were starting to squirm around in their chairs, obviously ready to get down and see what else they could get into. "Then let's take these dishes in the house and we'll go to the park."

Dishes inside and the house closed up, they went out the front door. Billy watched the boys as they climbed into the backseat of Darryl's car, fastening their seatbelts, and they rode through town, pulling into the drive and parking near a small pavilion. The boys climbed out and looked everywhere. They didn't know what they wanted to do first. There was a creek filled with geese and ducks, a huge play area with swings, a massive climbing fort, and of course the water itself. Taking their hands, Billy led them toward the play area. Pulling their hands away, they raced ahead, disappearing into the fort.

Billy felt Darryl's hand brush his as they approached the play structure. Billy waved when he saw Davey's head sticking out one of the battlement windows, and Donnie stuck his head out of the next one, his little hands waving to beat the band. "Have fun," Darryl called out to the twins, and Billy felt himself being gently led toward the swings around the side.

"Have you been here before? It's within walking distance." Darryl snagged a swing, and Billy sat in the one next to him.

"No. We weren't here long before Dad died, and since then, we've been doing everything we could just to survive." He saw the boys running across a bridge before climbing the stairs to the slide. "I wish I'd have known this was here. They need to get out and do normal things with other kids." Billy turned to Darryl and saw him begin to swing, using his feet to push off. As he watched, Darryl stopped his movement and jumped off his swing.

"I think it's time you had some fun too." Darryl got behind him and began to push. Higher and higher he began to swing, his stomach hopping and jumping every time. God, it was fun. As he moved, he saw Davey running over, pointing to him. Darryl moved away and set him on the other swing and began to push. Donnie hurried over, too, not one to be left out. Billy slowed his swing and got off. Placing his brother on the seat, he pushed him until dueling choruses of "higher, higher" competed with laughter for attention.

"I'm done," Billy heard Donnie call, and he slowed the swing to a stop. "Can we see the birdies?" He pointed toward the creek running along the edge of the park.

"They're ducks and geese," he corrected gently, and Donnie began running over. Billy barely kept up, but they were both passed by Darryl carrying a squealingly happy Davey. Billy caught up to the youngster just in time. "One of these days, your pants are gonna rip and you're going to go in the water headfirst," he scolded lightly, with Donnie completely ignoring him.

A young girl and her father stood down the way, throwing bread at the ducks. As they approached, the girl's dad gave each of the boys a slice of the bread, and all three kids had a field day trying to make the ducks fat. Billy stepped back, standing beside Darryl, watching his brothers. "It's so good to see them happy. Thank you." He looked at Darryl and desperately wanted to kiss him right there. There hadn't been much joy in their lives for a while, and something as simple as feeding the ducks meant so much to all of them. But Darryl slipped his arms around him, giving him a near-hug that was almost as good.

Once the bread was gone, the little girl waved goodbye and walked back to the car with her father. They waved goodbye as the boys shouted, "Thank you!" to the retreating tail lights. The boys looked at both of them as if to say, "Didn't you bring any?" before running back across the grass toward the play area.

"This was a wonderful idea; you made them so happy."

"What about you?" Darryl replied softly, walking next to him, a hand touching his arm. "Are you happy?"

Billy couldn't stop the smile from bursting onto his face. "I am."

"Good." Darryl led them toward a picnic table in the shade of the trees that lined the park, sitting next to him on the bench, their body heat mixing in the coolness of the shade. Billy felt himself shiver a little, and then Darryl tugged him closer, his body warming. "I'm glad you're having a good time, and I'm hoping they wear themselves out. They do still take naps, don't they?"

Billy raised his head from where he'd rested it on Darryl's shoulder. The man's deep, rich scent, mixed with the earthy aromas of the forest, was beginning to make him excited. "Yes, they do."

"Thank God, because what I really want is some time alone with you." Darryl moved his lips so close, Billy could feel their heat. "Want that very much."

Billy nodded slowly and felt himself swallow as he heated under Darryl's gaze. No one had ever looked at him the way Darryl was right now, like he was the main course at a buffet. "I want that too." Billy thought he could feel Darryl's lips brush his, but shouts and calls pulled their attention back to the play area. Both boys were running and playing happily, but it was a reminder to Billy that he had to keep his focus on them. He couldn't lose himself in Darryl, and that would suddenly be so easy for him to do. "Do you think it's time we thought about lunch? The boys are probably getting hungry, and after all this fresh air, once they've eaten, they'll probably go right to sleep for a while."

Darryl looked up and found the boys climbing over a rope bridge. "Davey, Donnie, five minutes." Billy began to chuckle softly. From their expressions, you'd have thought he'd just taken away the last toy on earth. "Billy and I will bring you back."

Davey ran over with Donnie following right behind. "You pwomise?" His little face looked so earnest, like it was just too good to be true.

"Of course," Darryl said with a smile that warmed Billy's heart. "Now play for the last few minutes and we'll go get lunch."

They ran back, and Billy sat and watched them, wondering what he'd ever done to bring this nice man into all their lives. It was almost too good to be true.

"What's wrong?" Darryl looked into his eyes. "You're suddenly so tense."

"I could get used to having you around, and it sort of scares me," Billy replied honestly.

"Why?"

"Because what if you're not? Around, I mean."

"I think it's a little early for me to start making promises, but I will tell you that I don't plan on going anywhere."

Billy figured that was all he could hope for and lifted himself off the bench, walking toward the play area. "Come on, boys. Time for lunch." To his surprise, they came with smiles, running up to both of them and babbling about all the things they had done and what they wanted to do the next time they came. The two men listened and replied enthusiastically before herding them toward the car.

Darryl drove them to McDonald's, and they got out, the boys racing for the doors. "I take it they know what McDonald's is?" Darryl said with a grin.

"They do, although they haven't been very often."

"Well, let's get them and us fed. I know it's terrible of me to say, but there are times I just crave a Big Mac." Darryl leaned close conspiratorially. "But for God's sake, don't tell Maureen—she'll never let me hear the end of it."

Billy ushered the boys to a table while Darryl ordered and brought a tray laden with food and set it on the table, passing out everyone's order. The boys continued jabbering as they stuffed chicken nuggets and French fries into their mouths. Billy noticed that Darryl had only gotten fries for the boys, and Billy figured it was the chef's French fry snobbery at work. He did his best to hide his smirk while eating his salad. It didn't take long to reduce the tray of food to empty wrappers and boxes, but they really knew it was time to go when Donnie slid under the table and began running toward the Ronald McDonald statue and decided he wanted to climb it. Bundling the boys back into the car, Darryl drove them back through town, pulling into the Walmart parking lot..

"I thought if we were going to take the boys in the car, they need to have booster seats," Darryl said once they were parked. "I'll run in and get them if you want to wait in the car with these two hooligans." Darryl turned around, giving each of the boys a tickle and getting a high-pitched, delighted giggle in return.

"But I…." Billy couldn't really afford them, but the idea that Darryl knew they'd need the seats and cared enough to get them was really nice.

"I'll be right back." Darryl leaned across the seat, giving Billy a quick kiss, silencing his protest, before opening his door, hurrying toward the entrance. Billy played I Spy with the boys until Darryl returned opening the boxes and installing the seats for the boys before they headed for Darryl's house.

By the time they arrived back at Darryl's, clouds had begun to roll in, and some of the day's warmth began to dissipate. He and the boys followed Darryl inside. The man opened the hall closet and pulled out two large metal trucks. "I played with these when I was a kid." The boys' eyes went wide and they knelt on the floor, immediately enthralled by the yellow scoop shovel and blue dump truck with their levers and pulleys that made everything move.

"What do you say?" Billy prompted, and both boys got up and gave Darryl a hug, telling him thank you before flopping back onto the floor to play with their immeasurable bounty.

"Let's go into the living room," Darryl prompted, and Billy followed him, sitting on the sofa.

"Can we go outside?" Davey asked as he came into the living room, carrying the dump truck in both hands.

Billy looked out the window and saw dark clouds building to the west. "I think it's going to rain."

Davey looked disappointed, but he didn't say anything.

"You can play on the floor in the hallway," Darryl said in consolation.

"But don't bang the trucks against the walls," Billy added as Davey smiled and walked away, joining Donnie in the hall. Soon the house was filled with the sounds of truck engines, brakes, and even the beep-beeps when they backed up.

"They're something else," Darryl said as he brought in two glasses of wine, setting them on the coffee table and taking a seat next to Billy on the sofa. They could hear the boys playing, but the back of the sofa provided a certain measure of privacy. "And so is their brother."

Billy felt Darryl's arms slide around him, and he looked into the older man's eyes as their lips got closer together. Billy ran his tongue along his upper lip, and then Darryl's lips took its place. Warm, firm, and tasting of rich wine, Darryl kissed him. It wasn't possessive or hard but filled with the urge for more. Billy made a soft sound, and Darryl understood it as permission, because the lips firmed against his, the kiss deepening, stealing the younger man's breath away. Billy could barely think, his mind short-circuiting. The sounds of trucks and children faded into the background, replaced by the excited beating of his heart. He was being kissed, a real kiss, by someone who wanted him and liked him.

Slowly, Billy pulled back, and the here and now returned. To his relief, Darryl looked into eyes deeply and then nipped his lower lips gently as a hand cradled his head. Then Billy was being kissed again, this time deeply, with a hardness and passion that stole his breath away. He placed his hands on Darryl's shoulders to steady himself as his mind reeled and swirled. Then he was falling—well, not falling exactly, but it felt like it until cushions rested against his back and Darryl's firm weight pressed onto him.

"I love those little sounds you make deep in your throat," Darryl whispered as he sucked on one of Billy's ears.

Billy giggled softly as a hand slid under his shirt, caressing his ticklish ribs. "We can't do this here."

"I know." He felt Darryl's weight lessen, and the man sat up, helping Billy do the same before handing him a glass of wine. Billy sipped a little and rested against Darryl's firm body, snuggling into the warmth as the first drops of rain pelted the front windows.

The house grew quiet, and Billy set down his glass before finding out what his brothers were up to. He found them in the downstairs bedroom peering out the window into the backyard. "Do the fish like the rain?" Donnie asked, pointing toward the pond.

Billy heard movement by the door and saw Darryl standing in the doorway. Davey yawned, and both he and Donnie followed. Darryl knew what that meant and turned down the covers on the bed. Billy removed the boys' shoes and settled them on the mattress. "When you wake up, we'll get ice cream," Darryl promised as their eyes drifted closed.

Leaving quietly, Billy cracked open the door and—"Ooof!"— he found himself nearly bouncing off Darryl, except strong arms held him in place for a few seconds before guiding them across the hall. "I use this as sort of a den." Opening the door, Billy gaped into the dark room with exposed brick walls. The door closing behind them, he was guided toward a huge, deep sofa, and they practically fell on it together, their lips meeting sometime during the tumble.

Their lips dueled, and Billy felt Darryl's hands slide under his shirt, pushing it up.

Darryl's head lifted away, and then those hot lips and tongue slid down his throat before sliding around one of his nipples, and Billy felt his back arch and his legs begin to throb as he thrust his chest closer. "God, you're responsive," Darryl moaned softly against Billy's skin, the hot breath sliding over the now cool, wet skin.

"Is that bad?" Billy was suddenly afraid he was doing something wrong. He was so excited he couldn't stop his legs from vibrating, and his dick felt like it was going to explode in his pants.

Darryl's head lifted, and their eyes met. "No way. It's the hottest thing ever." Darryl punctuated his feelings by sucking on a nipple, hands around Billy's back, holding him in his strong arms. When Darryl licked his way down Billy's stomach, the younger man began to giggle, but that stopped as soon as a hot tongue swirled in his belly button before licking a line just above the waistband of his jeans. "I've got you. Just enjoy and relax as best you can."

With those moaned words, Billy went with it, giving his body over to Darryl, who seemed to know how to play it like a fine instrument. He could hardly believe the things he was feeling. A small suck on his nipples made him shake. A lick down his side made his dick jump in his pants, which now seemed a full size too small, and when Darryl lifted his arms above his head, licking and kissing down beneath his arm to his nipple, he nearly came in his pants.

"Sorry, babe, but you need to keep it down."

Billy lifted his head through the haze of ecstasy Darryl had him in. "Oh." He'd done something wrong.

"Don't get me wrong. Those noises are so sexy, but I don't want to wake the boys." Darryl winked at him like he was going to be very naughty. "At least not until I'm done with you." Billy felt Darryl's hands open his belt and pop the button on his jeans. Then that tongue slid into the small opening like a hot, wet branding iron against his skin.

"Darryl." The head popped up again, and he got a lascivious grin as the hands slipped away, and then Darryl's shirt lifted and slid off before dropping to the floor. Billy's eyes followed it but snapped back as Darryl's tongue went back to work and he felt warm skin against his.

He let his hands roam, raking them along Darryl's wide back as he felt his pants slip open and lips run along his length. Even through his underwear, he could feel the heat, and he thrust forward, jamming himself against Darryl's face as he stifled a small cry. Then Darryl jumped off him and Billy looked up at him, wondering what he'd done. Had he hurt him somehow?

Darryl tugged him to his feet, Billy's jeans puddling around his ankles before he could grab them. Before he could bend down to pull them up, he felt Darryl's shoulder on his chest, and he was being lifted. "Hey," he cried softly as he got a great view of Darryl's back and butt. "What are you doing?" He reached down and grabbed a cheek.

"If we're going to do this, I want to do it right." They began to move through the house, but all Billy saw was the moving floor and Darryl's butt flexing as he walked. Stairs appeared, and they began moving up, then more floor, a door closing, and finally he was flung on the bed, bouncing a few times before his pants were tugged off his feet. His underwear followed unceremoniously.

Billy's first instinct was to hide. He was skinny and thin. "What do you want to see me for?"

Darryl's lips appeared in his line of sight, and hands slid over his skin. "Because you're beautiful."

"I am not. I'm all scrawny and pasty." His argument cut off as fingers circled around his length.

"Whoever told you that was full of crap," Darryl told him, and Billy swallowed, not really believing it. His dad had told him all the time that he was too small and took after his mother way too much. "You are absolutely"—the hand around him began to stroke gently, and he thought he was going to come unglued—"beautiful. Especially when you do that...."

"What?" Billy asked breathlessly as Darryl began stroking hard and faster. A hand slid under his butt, and he began to thrust, moving himself through those fingers. He could feel pressure building inside, and Billy knew he couldn't possibly last much longer.

"Come for me," Darryl said almost under his breath, though it was as if he'd shouted it. The pressure around and inside him was too much, and Billy cried out and stiffened as he came in ropes all over Darryl's hand.

Billy collapsed onto the bed, as limp as a rag doll. Slowly, he let his eyes open and saw Darryl's brilliant smile shining back at him. "See, I told you." Billy couldn't answer, and his heart decided to take Darryl's word for it. Soft lips met his, and Darryl held him tight, their bodies pressed together.

"But what about you?" Billy began to squirm, pushing Darryl onto his back, looking down at the older man.

"Why don't you undress me?"

Billy grinned and decided that turnabout was definitely fair play. Leaning forward, he ran his tongue over a small, hard nipple, doing the same things that Darryl had done to him before pulling open Darryl's belt and sliding down the zipper. Darryl arched his back, and Billy pulled the pants off his legs before dropping them to the floor. Darryl's cock jutted out of the top of his briefs, and Billy smiled as he tugged away the white cotton.

Sliding his hand tentatively along Darryl's skin, he suddenly found himself unsure of what to do. He'd wondered for days what Darryl looked like without his clothes, and now he was getting to see. The problem was that he couldn't decide what to touch first: strong chest; flat stomach; thick, full cock. *Duh.* Reaching out, he wrapped his hand around Darryl's length and slid gently along the skin. He wanted to give the man everything he'd given him, but he wasn't sure what to do. Finally, he decided to do what he liked and began stroking slowly with one hand while he teased the weighty balls with the other.

Darryl's eyes were closed, his mouth hanging open in an expression of happy bliss. "It's been so long. Feels so good." Darryl began to squirm on the bed, and Billy began stroking faster as he watched Darryl's expressions change. He didn't know exactly what those expressions were, but he knew what they meant. Darryl's hips started thrusting gently, and Billy went with the timing, listening as Darryl made this chorus of small noises punctuated with groans of encouragement. "Can't hold out."

"Don't. I want you to come. Show me what I looked like." That must have been the right thing to say, because Darryl's mouth fell open and he stiffened, coming onto his chest and all over Billy's hand.

Billy slid his hand away and reached for a tissue, cleaning himself and his lover off before resting on the bed. Darryl rolled over, pulling him close, kissing him softly. "Did I look like that too?"

"I'm sure you looked much better," Darryl replied as he kissed Billy's neck.

Billy let his eyes drift shut, figuring it would be okay to rest for a few minutes. Darryl's soft breathing told Billy he'd drifted off, and Billy's body desperately wanted to follow right along, but he fought it.

"Where are you going?" Darryl asked, eyes still closed, as Billy rolled away and began getting up.

"The boys will be up soon, and I don't want them wondering where I am," Billy replied. But before he could get up, Darryl grabbed him around the waist, tugging him back onto the bed. Billy found himself giggling as Darryl blew a raspberry on his stomach.

"I'll let you go if you make me a promise first."

"What kind of promise?" He stopped giggling but continued smiling.

"Stay here tonight."

Billy stilled, looking at Darryl in surprise. "You want me to stay with you?"

"Yes. I want to hold you all night. We can listen to the rain and make love in the middle of the night, and I'll make sure you aren't late for work in the morning."

"You will, huh?" Billy teased as he settled on the bed, Darryl's warmth cocooning him.

"Yeah, I will." Darryl settled on his side, and Billy looked up into those kind brown eyes.

"Am I some charity case you're taking pity on?"

"Where did that come from?" Billy felt Darryl tense against him. "Have I ever treated you as though I pitied you?"

"No. But I can't figure out what you see in me."

"How about if I just see you and I like you?" Darryl hugged him close, touching him from chest to toe. "You are not to be pitied but admired. Can't you see that? You're willing to do whatever you can for your brothers, and that's pretty special."

"They're my brothers."

"I know, but you'd do the same thing for them even if they weren't. And that's what I like about you." Darryl leaned close, capturing Billy's lips, kissing him hard. Darryl could have talked until he was blue, but those lips conveyed in a simple kiss everything Billy needed to know.

"We should still get up."

"I know. But you haven't answered my question. Will you stay?" Darryl spun the words so softly, almost delicately.

"Yes." Billy smiled, and Darryl kissed him again as the sound of small feet carried up the stairs. With a smile on his just-kissed lips, Billy got out of bed and pulled on his clothes. By the time they were both dressed and heading down the stairs, the footsteps had been replaced by the sound of trucks.

"Are we really gonna get ice cream?" Donnie looked up at them from where he was playing.

"Yup." Darryl ran over and lifted the little boy into the air, flying him around the room. "Just as soon as you're ready."

"I ready," Davey piped up, racing for the front door. Darryl put Donnie down, and he zoomed out of the room on his brother's heels.

"Boys, I have to tell you something." They both stopped and turned toward him. "Darryl asked us to stay at his house tonight. Is that okay?"

They both stood quietly, and Billy could almost see their little minds working. "You mean like a sleepover?" Davey asked, eyes wide.

"Yes, like a sleepover." He turned to Darryl, wondering if this was what the man truly had in mind when he extended the invitation.

"Okay." They both walked to the front door. "Can we get ice cream now?"

"Yes, we can get you a treat," Darryl said as they opened the door. Thankfully, it had stopped raining. As they stepped outside, Darryl leaned close to Billy. "They can have their treat now, and we can have ours later."

Billy nudged Darryl's shoulder, smiling as they got in the car.

CHAPTER SEVEN

"IF YOU keep grinning like that, your face will stay that way and you'll look like the Joker," Maureen teased from her workstation. "I take it things with Billy are going well." She turned on the mixer and set her timer before walking to where Darryl was preparing for the lunch service.

"Yeah, they are. The last month has been the best I can remember."

"Even better than opening the restaurant?" she asked sheepishly.

"Yeah." Darryl nodded his head, smiling like a fool. "Who knew hiring a new waiter could change everything so quickly. I mean…." He was stammering—that hadn't come out quite how he'd wanted.

"I know exactly what you mean, and for the record, it's a good thing. For the last month or so, you've been so happy." She stepped back to her station and turned off the mixer. "It's just good to see." Maureen began scraping down the sides of the bowl before turning on the mixer again. "So have you decided to promote Sebastian?"

Darryl felt another smile coming on. "I did it last night. He's really stepped up, and he deserves it. You should have heard him."

"Good for you." She went back to work, and the kitchen became quiet.

Darryl's thoughts roamed to Billy and the boys. They'd spent a lot of time together since that Sunday in the park a month earlier. When Billy was around, he was happy, and when he wasn't, Darryl spent most of his time looking forward to seeing him again. Finishing up the vegetables, he checked the clock and walked to the door, peering into the dining room, where Sebastian was already hard at work checking that everything was ready. "Have you seen Billy?" It was getting close to opening time.

Sebastian shook his head, looking concerned. "I haven't seen him, and he's never late."

"I know." Darryl let the door close and wandered back through the kitchen to his office. Or more accurately, what had once been his office. Stepping inside, he shook his head. How things had changed. His desk was where it had always been, but the rest of the room looked like a day care center. There were crayon pictures on the walls, toys stacked in the corner, and even a television with a DVD player on a small stand.

"Those boys have really taken over in here, haven't they?" Maureen's voice held nothing but amusement. "I think those boys and their brother have taken over someplace else as well, haven't they?"

Darryl nodded; he couldn't deny it. His heart was full, and it was wonderful. "I wonder where he is."

The back door opened and banged closed, and a few seconds later, the boys raced into the room. Both he and Maureen were given big hugs before they turned on the TV and settled on the old futon. Darryl looked toward the door and saw Billy walk in. Something was definitely wrong. His usual smile was absent, but it was the defeated look in his eyes that made Darryl worry. "What's wrong?" Darryl asked.

"I'm opening up," Sebastian called from the kitchen doors.

Billy shook his head in answer to Darryl's question. "I've got to get to work." Billy smiled, but it was hollow.

Darryl looked at the boys to see if he could get a clue as to what was bothering Billy, but they were happily watching Sponge Bob, and nothing with them seemed out of the ordinary in the least.

Billy left the room, and Darryl followed him, putting his hand on his shoulder to stop him a second. "Can we talk about what's wrong?"

The printer in the kitchen began spitting out orders. "We need to get to work," was all Billy said before he walked away and out into the dining room. Darryl started on the orders, and soon he was almost too busy to think—almost. Sometimes he got so engrossed in his work that he'd forget something was bothering Billy, but then he'd see him, the worry showing plainly on his face, making Darryl's insides twist each and every time. "What could have happened?" he asked himself under his breath.

Billy hadn't stayed over last night. After work yesterday, they'd both been so tired that they'd just gone home. That was how it was most nights. When they'd parted last night, Billy had kissed him as though nothing was wrong, and now he was obviously upset. He didn't think it could be anything he'd done, but he didn't want to see the man he loved…. Darryl stopped in the middle of his task, not moving, the notion hitting him in the stomach.

"What's wrong?" Maureen asked from behind him.

"Nothing," he replied, probably a little too quickly. "Just a little worried, I guess." He pulled his mind back to the task at hand and returned to cooking. It was always the one thing that could take his mind off everything else. Well, up until today, that was. The look on Billy's face just wouldn't leave his mind.

During a short lull in the orders, he wandered back to where the boys were. They were crouched on the floor around the kid-sized table Maureen had brought in, heads down, drawing pictures and coloring. Without disturbing them, he walked back to his area and returned to his work.

Finally, the lunch orders slowed down, and after filling what seemed like a million of them today, Darryl took a deep breath and began the task of cleaning up. Billy walked into the kitchen, his customer smile quickly fading. Darryl could take no more; his curiosity and concern wouldn't let him wait another second. "Let's go out back and talk." Billy looked like he didn't want to go, but Darryl wasn't about to take no for an answer.

The back door clanged closed behind them, and Darryl waited to see if Billy would spill what had him so obviously upset. "I got a letter this morning. They passed it under the door of the apartment last evening. It seems the building has been sold, and it's going to be completely refurbished."

"That means they'll be fixing up your apartment." Billy shook his head slowly in response. "Doesn't it?" he added as an afterthought.

"No, it means we have ninety days to find another place to live." Billy looked as though he was about to cry. "I can barely afford this place, and only because it's the cheapest place in town." Billy was completely crestfallen. "I just filled out the applications to get the boys enrolled in school here, and it looks like we may need to move again."

"Can they do that to you? What about your lease?" Darryl asked.

"I don't have one." Billy felt so stupid. "They never offered or asked for one, and I was so relieved to find something that didn't cost a fortune." Now he and the boys could be out on the street.

"Wait a minute. You're moving away?"

"I may have to unless I can find a place to live that we can afford." Billy's body went lax, and he leaned against the side of the building.

"How much sleep did you get last night?" Darryl gently tugged the smaller man into his arms. "I'd guess you barely slept at all."

"I spent most of the night staring at the ceiling wondering what I was going to do." Billy returned his hug, and Darryl felt his breath against the skin of his neck.

The thought of Billy leaving was too much for him. "Why don't you come live with me?" Darryl ran his hand through Billy's soft hair.

"I can't ask you to do that," Billy replied as he pulled back from their hug, looking at Darryl with disbelieving eyes.

"You didn't ask me—I offered." Darryl let his arms fall to his sides as Billy backed away.

"I know we've spent a lot of time at your house, but do you really know what you're offering?" Billy asked, a note of hope in his voice. "There's no way I can ever hope to pay our fair share of a house like yours, and are you sure you want me and Davey and Donnie living with you full time?" The words came tumbling out. "They'll get attached to you, and if...."

"Yes, I'm sure. I love you, Billy." Darryl said the words softly, and they had the desired effect. Billy's tirade stopped in its tracks, and he stood there with his mouth open.

"You love me?" Billy's eyes widened, and he swallowed hard.

Darryl nodded, smiling. "Yes." Then he stepped forward. "And I want you and the boys to come live with me." Darryl held out his hand and waited. "Before I met the three of you, my life was nothing but work. Now I look forward to every minute I get to spend with you."

Billy finally lifted his hand and placed it in Darryl's. "We can't live with you out of charity."

"It isn't charity." Darryl tightened the grip just a bit, running his thumb over the back of Billy's hand. "I love you."

"But what if you hate me later? What if you decide you don't want us anymore?"

"Are you willing to try, then?" Darryl asked softly, and Billy nodded. "Then you can pay me the same rent you were paying at the Molly." Darryl pulled Billy into a hug, his heart swelling with joy.

"I just have one more question."

Darryl began to laugh softly. "Just one?"

"Yeah." Billy looked into his eyes, smirking slightly. "Where do you want me to sleep?"

Darryl felt a sudden wave of insecurity. "Well, I'd dreamed you'd want to sleep with me. You don't have to, you know. That's not a requirement. But I would hope it would be a pleasure. I know it would be for me." God, just the thought of seeing Billy's bright smile before going to sleep and waking to those deep eyes every morning was enough to get him excited right there in the alley.

Billy nodded slightly, and Darryl hugged him tighter, running his fingers through his hair. He wanted to dance for joy, he was so happy. "Can I tell the boys?" Billy's voice was kind of muffled.

"You can tell anyone you like," Darryl replied, still smiling as he guided them toward the door. Billy gave him another hug and then pulled open the door, rushing inside. Darryl followed him and stood in the doorway as Billy explained things to the boys, who both shrugged and went back to their drawing.

"I guess I was hoping for a little more than that," Billy said as he joined Darryl in the hallway.

"How many times have they moved in the last few years?" Darryl asked as he got back to his station. Kelly had already done much of the cleanup and continued bustling around him, getting things ready for dinner. He thanked her softly as Billy watched him over the counter.

"Three or four, I guess."

"Then it's probably nothing special anymore when they're told they have to move."

"I suppose you're right. Dad never seemed to stay in one place very long. He always said he liked to wander." Billy bit his upper lip slightly. "But I think that after Mom died, he didn't care as much about anything anymore, even us. He'd get a job and keep it for a few months. I know he tended to drink a little too much sometimes, and he was one of those people who'd be late for his own funeral." Billy's lip started to tremble a little, and Darryl stopped what he was doing, walking around the counter. "I always wondered what I had done wrong, and I think he blamed the boys for her death. She didn't die right after they were born, but he always told me that she never recovered from the complications and trauma of giving birth to the twins."

Darryl tugged Billy close, holding him as he looked toward the office door, the sound of the television and little boy laughter drifting into the kitchen. *How could anyone blame those kids for anything?* "Sometimes these things happen, and no one's to blame."

Billy lifted his head away from Darryl's chest and wiped his eyes. "I know, but I wish he had taken more interest in the boys. Even when he was alive, I did most of the work raising them. They may be my brothers, but they're probably as close to having my own children as I'm ever going to get."

"Darryl, Julio should be in soon. I can handle the dinner service with him tonight if you want." He looked up and saw the excited look on Kelly's face.

"Thank you." He could almost see her energy ramp up, and he was more than grateful for her offer. Billy was almost dead on his feet, and Darryl had been distracted all afternoon. "Let's get you and the boys back to the house."

"I'm sorry," Billy mumbled against him. "I should just take the boys back to the apartment and not get in your way."

"You're not in the way. Kelly and Julio can handle things just fine." Darryl realized just how true that statement was. They could handle things. He'd done a good job training them both, and for the first time, Darryl realized that there was something—someone—in his life more important than the restaurant. "You get the boys ready, and I'll finish up a few things. Then we'll go." Billy seemed to be getting more and more lethargic, and he watched him slowly walk to the office before heading through to the dining room.

The servers and bussers were finishing in the dining room, and Sebastian came right over. "Is Billy okay? He didn't seem like himself today."

"He'll be fine," Darryl soothed. The two men had become friends, and he heard genuine concern in Sebastian's voice. "I'm taking him home to rest. Julio and Kelly will handle things tonight."

"I've got plenty of help out here, so we should be just fine," Sebastian interjected. "Take care of him." Sebastian stopped, and Darryl felt his intense gaze for a second. "Something's happened between you two hasn't it?"

Darryl felt himself grinning like an idiot. "Billy and the boys are going to move in with me."

Sebastian returned the smile. "Good. He needs someone to care for him. I get the impression that he hasn't gotten much care or tenderness other than Davey and Donnie in a while."

Darryl nodded in response. Billy was one of the most caring, loving people Darryl had ever met.

Sebastian continued, almost like he was reading his thoughts, "Maybe that's why he's so attentive to everyone else, hoping that some of it will come back to him."

Damn, the man was observant. "I think you're right, and I plan to make sure it does." Darryl slapped Sebastian on the shoulder. "I'll see you tomorrow."

"Okay," Sebastian replied as his attention shifted. "Not that table, push the other two together… perfect, thank you." Sebastian's attention shifted back to him. "Don't worry about anything, we can handle it." And Darryl knew they could. "We'll call if anything comes up."

"Thanks, Sebastian."

"No problem," the man replied as he moved away to help the server with the tables, and Darryl went back into the kitchen. Julio had arrived, and he and Kelly had their heads together planning the service, just like he'd taught them. Letting go of some of the trepidation that gripped him whenever he wasn't working, he said goodbye, and they both nodded before returning to work.

"You ready?" Darryl asked as he stepped into the office. Billy was sitting on the futon, already half asleep, with a book in his hand, trying to read to the boys.

"Yeah." He barely looked up.

"Come on, boys. Let's get in the car."

"Are we going to your house?" Davey asked.

"No, we're going to your house," Darryl corrected with a smile. "You're going to live there too, remember?"

"Uh-huh," Donnie replied for both of them, and they got up. Billy closed the book, getting to his feet and shuffling to the door.

Darryl hung back, watching them all: Davey and Donnie skipping ahead, racing each other to the car, and Billy shuffling along behind then. Darryl realized that all three of them had completely stolen his heart. In a month, those two boys had him wrapped around their fingers, and Billy had a tight grip on his heart. It didn't matter so much that he'd told Billy he loved him and the younger man hadn't said the words back. He had hoped Billy would feel comfortable enough to say the words, but Darryl could tell by the way Billy looked at him and responded to his touch that Billy had to be feeling the same things he was, even if he couldn't bring himself to say the words.

"Can we stop and get our toys?" Davey asked.

"Please?" The way Donnie said the word was so cute. "I want my trucks and Herbie."

"Okay, we'll make a quick stop to get your things." Darryl unlocked the car, and the boys climbed in the backseat, jabbering constantly as he and Billy got in front. "It won't take long, I promise."

Billy nodded a little and smiled weakly. The man was dead on his feet, and Darryl wanted to get him home in a comfortable bed so he could sleep. He'd known worried and sleepless nights—Darryl had spent many of them when he was hoping and trying to get the loan to open Café Belgie.

Darryl drove to Billy's apartment and they went up, getting the things the boys and Billy would need, before heading to Darryl's house. Parking out front, he unlocked the door, the boys rushing inside and through the house. "They're fascinated by your fish," Billy said as Darryl guided him into the house.

"I guess so." Darryl grinned. "They told me they named one Gordon and the other one Anna," Darryl told Billy as they made their way upstairs and into his room, their room. Billy sat on the edge of the bed, and Darryl helped his lover undress. Over the past month, this process had usually been very erotic, but today, it became an exercise in caring. Pulling down the bedding, Darryl let Billy lie down before making sure he was comfortable. "Just sleep, love. I'll watch the boys. There's nothing to worry about."

"You really love me?" Billy's voice sounded small, filled with sleep.

"Yes, I do." He leaned forward, lightly kissing those sweet lips.

"Good, 'cause I love you too." Billy returned his kiss, and Darryl felt his heart soar in his chest. Brushing Billy's hair out of his eyes, he stood up and quietly left the room, cracking the door. Taking a last peek inside, he saw that his lover was already asleep, a small smile on his face.

Downstairs, Darryl found the boys in the backyard, playing with their trucks. Making sure they were okay, he went out front, unloaded the car, and brought their things inside.

"Would you like me to read you a story?" he asked from the entrance to the backyard once everything was in its temporary place.

"Clifford!" Davey called back.

"I want Babar," Donnie argued, both of them leaving their trucks where they were, racing toward where Darryl stood.

"I'll read both of them if you'll put your toys away." Darryl smiled as the boys rushed to clean up and then clomped through the house behind him and into the back sitting room. Picking up the books he'd left downstairs, he let each boy pick one and then sat on the sofa with a five-year-old on either side of him. "Clifford the Big Red Dog." Both boys settled down to listen as Darryl opened the book and began to read.

By the time both stories were done, Darryl sat between two sleeping kids, each leaning against him. He'd barely started the second book when first Donnie and then Davey had shifted on the sofa, curling up against his side. Getting up slowly, he resettled each of the boys and covered them with the throw from the back of the sofa. Reaching into the bag of toys he'd set aside, Darryl found a stuffed bear and a hippo. As he set them next to the boys, the plush animals were immediately cuddled to them in their sleep.

Leaving the room, he climbed the stairs and went to where Billy was sleeping. Slipping off his shoes, he climbed beneath the covers, and Billy immediately curled up to him without waking. Kissing Billy's forehead, he closed his eyes. One crisis had been averted, and he'd actually gotten Billy sleeping in his bed out of it. He hoped that all their crises ended this way.

CHAPTER EIGHT

BILLY woke to Darryl spooned to his back, his soft breath against his skin, light just starting to filter in through the windows. He smiled to himself as he remembered Darryl making the boys dinner and then insisting they spend the night before helping him tuck the boys into the guest room bed. Pushing down the covers, he gently released Darryl's arm and began getting out of bed.

"Where do you think you're going?" Darryl's groggy voice floated to his ears as an arm tugged him back into the bed.

"We have to get the boys up and get ready for work." Billy giggled softly. It was the last thing he wanted to do. Being in bed with Darryl, snuggled up to him, was where he wanted to stay for the whole day, but the boys and work had other ideas.

"It's Sunday, remember?" Darryl wriggled his hips against Billy's butt. "So we don't have to get up, and if we're quiet, the boys will sleep for a while." Darryl's hand rubbed Billy's belly slowly, lips kissing his neck. It felt so good and comforting to be held. Darryl's languid kisses continued until Billy felt the bed shift and he was rolled onto his back, Darryl's body pressing him into the mattress, his weight solid and firm. The kisses continued, building in intensity, desire ratcheting up. "You taste so good." Darryl kissed him again, their tongues exploring. "You feel good too." Darryl's lips turned into a grin as his hardness slid against Billy's hip. "Really good."

Darryl's lips slipped away and found Billy's nipple, sliding and nipping at his skin. "Darryl!" Billy arched into the touch, hands sliding over Darryl's back. His hips thrust forward on their own, trying to get a purchase against Darryl's skin, but he just... couldn't... quite... get it.

"Just relax, hon." Darryl's head lifted slightly, lips finding his again. "I know we haven't done a lot together yet, but there is something I want to give you." Darryl's lips went back to their erotically delicious work, and Billy fought the urge to cry out whenever Darryl touched one of those spots that made his skin tingle and his head spin.

"What are you doing?" Billy asked through shallow panting breaths as Darryl continued kissing his way down his chest and stomach.

"I'm loving you, all of you."

Billy brought a finger to his mouth, biting on a knuckle as hot wetness surrounded his length, taking him deep and hard. He felt the air rush from his lungs, and every cell in his body cried out as Darryl's tongue did something that made his eyes roll back in his head. Then Darryl started to suck, and Billy felt hands slide under him, cupping his butt, encouraging him to move. That was all the invitation he needed. Arching his back again, he began moving, thrusting with abandon, and Darryl took it, giving him the most incredible experience he'd ever had. Then Darryl's lips pulled away, and Billy whined softly, his body thrusting. He'd been so close.

"Not quite yet," Darryl whispered as hands soothed along his skin.

"That's just mean," Billy whined softly.

"You won't think so in a minute," Darryl replied, lifting Billy's legs and guiding his knees to his chest. Billy wasn't so sure about this, but when Darryl's tongue slid along his skin, prodding his opening, Billy threw back his head and couldn't contain the small cry of bliss that escaped him. Hands cupped his cheeks, tongue searing his skin. Billy reached for his erection and began stroking in earnest, but one of Darryl's hands batted it away. "I'll take good care of you, just trust me."

Billy nodded slowly—he'd agree to just about anything to get Darryl to do that again. Billy felt a finger tease his opening before slipping inside him. He almost protested, but then his entire length was engulfed in wet heat and his ability to speak flew out the window along with all cognitive thought. The range of his senses narrowed to Darryl's touch and the small sounds that filled the room. Everything else shut off.

Billy's skin was on fire, and every movement Darryl made intensified the sensations. He let his head rock on the pillow, his hips moving back and forth, filling Darryl's mouth as his lover drove that finger deeper inside him. Suddenly, Darryl touched him somewhere magical, and stars flashed behind Billy's eyes. The pressure that had been building deep inside could no longer be contained, and his climax burst from him, gushing down Darryl's throat.

He hadn't felt Darryl swallow or even move from on top of him. All he felt were heaving breaths and small caresses that helped bring him back to himself. "Are you back with me?"

Billy managed to nod as he started catching his breath. "Uh-huh." Billy felt the bed shift, and then Darryl was holding him, caressing his skin and pulling him close. "What about you?" Billy felt mortified—in his pleasure he'd completely forgotten about Darryl.

"I came when you did. The look on your face when you came was so hot, I couldn't stop myself." Darryl's lips found his, and they kissed hard and long, caressing one another with their hands, their bodies sharing the warmth of love's glow.

Darryl reached to the foot of the bed and tugged up the covers, cocooning them in warmth, and Billy felt himself drift back into a relaxed, contented sleep, and it was only the sound of hurried feet on the floor followed by the bouncing on the bed only two little boys could cause that woke him.

"We're hungry, Uncle Dawwyl," Davey pronounced as they both climbed over them, giving out good morning hugs.

"Okay. You two go on downstairs, and I'll be down in a minute." Hurried little feet rushed away, the door banging closed behind them, and Billy felt Darryl slip out of bed, pulling on his clothes. "Rest for a while. I'll keep the rabble entertained, and after we eat, we'll get the rest of your things from the apartment."

Billy rolled over slowly, looking into Darryl's face. "The company that bought the building said they'd provide a moving allowance."

"Then we'll collect that today as well, and you can use it to get some things for yourself and the boys." Darryl buttoned his pants and slipped a T-shirt over his head before leaning forward for a kiss, which Billy happily gave. "I'll see you downstairs in a little while."

Billy watched as Darryl left the room. Everything in his life was so good right now. Darryl loved him and the boys, he had a nice place to live, a lot better than that dump he had been living in, and to top it off, he had a job he liked. He was tempted to jump on the bed like the boys. It was almost too good to be true. Allowing himself a little bounce, he actually giggled with glee before jumping out of the bed and hurrying to the bathroom.

Billy started the shower before turning to the sink to shave. Leaving the remnants of the shaving cream on his face, he stepped under the water and pulled the curtain closed. The water felt amazing on his skin as he stood unmoving under it, letting it cascade over him.

The sound of the curtain pulling back made him jump. Turning around, he saw an amazingly naked Darryl stepping into the tub. "The boys are happy with a bowl of cereal, so they're out eating where they can watch the fish, and I thought I'd join you. I know we don't have time for a repeat of this morning"—Darryl's arms wrapped around him—"but I thought we could at least be together."

Darryl picked up the bar of soap and began washing his shoulders, sliding down his chest before fingers wrapped around his dick, which hardened immediately under the touch. "I thought you said we don't have time." Billy's hips began to move on their own.

"I meant we don't have much time." Darryl tightened his grip, and Billy hissed between his teeth. "Yeah, that's it. Take what you need," Darryl cooed as Billy thrust harder, holding onto Darryl's shoulders for balance. "You look like a debauched angel when you come, you know that? So beautiful and all mine." Darryl kept talking, and Billy felt that his body was going to erupt any second. "No one else gets to see this, or feel this, only me, love, only me."

Billy gasped, his legs shaking, arms throbbing as he came, hanging on to Darryl for dear life. When his shocks stopped rippling through his body, he opened his eyes. A very hot and wet man stared at him, a look of delight on his face. Able to think again, Billy took the bar of soap and lathered his hands, letting them slide over the bigger man. He loved the way Darryl's chest muscles flexed and danced under his touch, the way his stomach tightened whenever his hands stroked over the ridges. He especially loved the way the corded muscles in the man's legs twisted and stretched when he ran his hands around to his butt, cupping the firm cheeks in his hands. "Now it's my turn," Billy whispered as he nipped Darryl's shoulders.

Lathering his hands again, he wound his fingers around Darryl's thick length and began his slow strokes, watching his eyes to make sure he was doing it right. Damn, from the look on that face, he was definitely doing it the way Darryl liked it. Eyes closed, mouth open, breath hitched, a soft moan. Twisting his fingers, Billy smiled as the moan increased to a soft cry. "You know things go both ways. You're mine, Darryl, and nobody else gets to see you like this. Legs jerking, breath held"—Billy leaned closer—"balls pulling tight." Billy ran his fingers along Darryl's perineum, and his lover's thrusting picked up its pace. "That's it, let me see it. Want to watch you."

"Billy!" Darryl cried as he came in white ropes onto Billy's hand.

The bigger man leaned back against the bathroom wall, breathing like he'd run a marathon. Once he'd recovered, Billy hugged him tight, kissing him gently beneath the hot spray.

Turning off the water, they got out and dried off quickly. Darryl went to dress, while Billy cleaned up the room before he, too, went into the bedroom. Dressing quickly, he followed Darryl down the stairs, watching the bigger man's butt flex in his jeans.

Billy immediately looked for the boys and found them still in the backyard, on their knees near the pond, little hands reaching for the water, Darryl's fencing working like a charm. The boys could see, but not get near the pond. "What are you two doing?"

"Fishing," Donnie responded, completely innocent. "We wanted to pet the fish."

Billy had to suppress a howl of laughter. "Fish don't like to be petted," he scolded lightly, and they stood up. "If you're done eating, put your dishes in the sink and get ready. We're going to the apartment today."

Davey made a face like he smelled something bad. "I don't want to. I wanna stay here." He stamped his foot in what looked like a little tantrum. "I don't wanna live there no more."

"We aren't. Uncle Darryl's taking us over there so we can get our stuff and bring it here," Billy explained, watching as both boys looked at him funny. "This is our home now. Me, Davey, Donnie, and Uncle Darryl."

"Forever. We don't gotta move anymore?" Davey's eyes narrowed suspiciously.

"Nope, we aren't moving anymore." Darryl brought out a tray with two plates and glasses. "So go get ready, and when we're done,

A TASTE OF LOVE

we'll get our things and bring them back here." They boys walked inside, and Billy followed behind, making sure they went upstairs before returning to the table and sitting next to Darryl.

Unfortunately, they had to eat in a bit of a hurry, and they took their dishes back inside, the boys watching television until they were finally all set to leave.

Once they got to the Molly and went upstairs, Billy unlocked the apartment door and stepped inside. Everything was as they'd left it.

"Why don't you start packing and I'll haul things downstairs?" Darryl offered.

"There really isn't that much here now." During the week, they'd made a number of trips, bringing most of the smaller things. "The furniture isn't worth bothering with," Billy said as he began stripping the beds.

"What do you want to do with it?" Darryl inquired as he helped the boys empty the last of their things into boxes.

"Just leave it. They can throw it all away." Billy didn't want any of it. What little they had, his dad had gotten at Goodwill or the curb, and it was practically falling apart anyway. Getting down on his hands and knees, he peered under his bed and reached beneath it, pulling out a metal box.

"What is that?" Darryl asked, looking over his shoulder.

"It was my dad's. I'd almost forgotten about it." Billy shook it a little. "The school needs copies of the boys' birth certificates, and I haven't been able to find them." He shook it again and tried to open the lid. "Maybe they're in here. It's locked, though." Billy started shaking it again. "It rattles a little but sounds sort of muffled."

"Let's take it with us. I've got some tools at the house. If we don't find the key, we'll break it open."

Billy nodded and set it down on the pile of things to take to the car.

It didn't take them long to finish packing up what little was there, and once the car was loaded, leaving just enough room in the backseat for the boys, they closed the door and locked it. Billy knocked on his neighbor's door to say goodbye, but he didn't get an answer. Shrugging to himself, he picked up the last box and took the stairs down. Dropping the keys at the manager's, he collected a check for his deposit refund as well as the moving allowance and left the building for the last time.

"You ready?" Darryl asked as Billy stood in front of the battered building.

"Yeah." He handed Darryl the last box and looked up at the scarred and weathered façade, saying goodbye to that part of his life. Then he turned and climbed into the car, not looking back as they pulled away.

At their new home—in Billy's mind it was now official, since all their stuff was here and the apartment was gone—they unloaded the car into the front room.

"What are you staring at?" Darryl came up behind him, putting his arms over his shoulders, resting his head against Billy's.

"My entire life up to now fits in"—he counted to himself—"twelve boxes, and most of that belongs to the boys."

"You know that doesn't matter, don't you?" Darryl's hand slid under Billy's shirt, and he shivered excitedly as the older man stroked his skin. "It's not what's in those boxes that matters, but what's in here." Darryl's hand tapped over his heart. "The rest is things, but this"—he tapped again—"is special."

"Sometimes I feel as though I'll never be able to contribute as much to you as you do to me."

"You contribute plenty just by being here." Darryl sucked lightly on Billy's ear. "Besides, not only are you cute, but you're tasty too." He nipped again as Billy began to laugh. "Let's get all this put away, have lunch, and then take the boys to the park for a while. They were so good throughout all this."

"Yeah, let's," Billy agreed, and he picked up the first box, taking it upstairs to the boys' room. Darryl had given them a room close to theirs. He'd insisted on getting them matching racecar beds, to their absolute, screaming delight. Opening the box, Billy took out the toys and placed them in the toy box in the corner before flattening the cardboard and taking it back downstairs.

When he stepped onto the landing, he heard Darryl reading about King Babar and Queen Celeste. Grabbing another armload of boxes, he bundled them upstairs. His clothes he hung in the closet Darryl had cleared for him, and he put away the rest of the boys' things.

After making two more trips, the last, lonely box sat just off the hall. Opening it, Billy pulled out a few pictures and his dad's metal box. "You ready for lunch?" Darryl called from the other room.

"We are!" came a chorus of small voices, followed by quick footsteps rushing toward the kitchen. "We're gonna help Uncle Darryl, Biwwy." He knew if Darryl got too much of their "help," they'd never get to eat, but he said nothing.

Returning to the box, he lifted out an old framed picture—his parents at their wedding. Looking around, he stood it on the mantel and stepped back. "You miss them, don't you?"

"Yeah. Dad could be"—he tried to find the right word—"hard and selfish sometimes, but I miss him."

Darryl walked to the mantel, picking up the faded photograph. "Your mother was beautiful." Darryl smiled. "Now I know where you get your looks." He set the picture back. "You really do look a lot like her."

Billy started at the picture, barely hearing what Darryl was saying. "Sorry?"

"I asked if the box was empty."

"Almost." Billy pulled out the last few pictures and set the empty box with the others, then returned to the room, picking up the metal box.

"Do you want to try to open that after lunch?"

Billy shook his head. "It can wait until after we go to the park." Leaving the room, he followed Darryl to the small kitchen. Billy really didn't think it fair that Darryl had to cook on his day off, so setting the box on one of the chairs, he found some space in the kitchen and helped his lover make lunch.

After eating and cleaning up, they drove to the park by way of the grocery store for a loaf of bread, and the boys spent much of the afternoon feeding the ducks and geese an entire loaf of bread, as well as playing and running. Billy and Darryl each brought along a book and spent a quiet afternoon watching the boys and reading on a blanket in the shade of one of the large trees. "This is the perfect way to spend a Sunday afternoon, here in the park, with you," Darryl whispered into Billy's ear as he set his book down on the blanket.

"I can think of something better." Billy smirked. "Try home, in bed, boys asleep…." Billy let his voice trail off suggestively as he went back to his book. Darryl's fingers wriggled up his side, sending him into fits of laughter as he twisted and squirmed away.

The boys ran over and flopped down on the blanket, getting into the act, and soon all of them were rolling around, laughing hysterically, as Davey and Donnie screamed with childish delight.

"We should get home," Billy pronounced with a smile. "I know two boys who need a bath before they go to bed." The groans were nearly deafening. "Get your things and go play for ten more minutes, then we'll need to go home." The boys raced off, and Billy relaxed back on the blanket, his eyes traveling up to the canopy of leaves above his head.

"Are you happy, Billy?" Darryl asked, settling next to him.

"Yes." He turned his head to look at Darryl. "Very happy." Letting his head roll back, he stared at the leaves and sky until it was time to leave.

At the house, they got a light dinner, and Billy nearly drowned giving Davey and Donnie their baths. They had water all over the bathroom from their playing and splashing. Drying them off, Billy got them in their pajamas and into bed. Darryl joined him in their bedroom, and they read stories before turning out the light.

"Let's go see what's in that box," Billy commented as they went down the stairs.

"Okay. The tools are in the basement." Darryl opened the door and turned on the light, and Billy got the box, joining him at a wooden worktable. "You don't care about the box, do you?"

"Nope, it's just a plain metal box. Let's pop it and see what's inside."

Darryl got a screwdriver and tried to work it under the lid, but it was too tight and wouldn't move. Getting a hammer, he fished in his tool box for a smaller screwdriver. Working it into the lock, he used it as a lever and tried to pop it. That didn't work either, but it seemed to loosen the lid. Working a screwdriver under it, they managed to pop it open with a little force and a few well-placed blows of the hammer.

Darryl handed the box to Billy, who lifted the now-battered lid. There appeared to be mostly papers inside. Lifting out the top set, Billy opened them and saw his parents' certificate of marriage. Setting it aside, he found birth certificates for himself, his mother, and his father. He also found his mother's death certificate. Beneath those, he found a packet of letters tied with a ribbon. They were addressed to his father, and Billy knew they had to be letters his mother had written him while he was in the service. Setting them aside to read later, he found a small box; inside was a wedding band and an engagement ring.

"Those must be your mother's," Darryl commented softly, and Billy nodded, unable to speak around the lump in his throat. Billy closed the box and held it for a second. For some reason, those small things made him feel closer to her. There was another box, slightly larger than the other, and Billy lifted it out, taking off the lid. Inside was a pin of what looked like a hummingbird. "That looks enameled," Darryl breathed, and Billy handed it to him so he could take a look. "It is, probably over gold." He handed it back to Billy. "It's really beautiful."

"She used to wear this whenever she got dressed up. She told me that my dad brought it back for her when he came home from the army. According to her, my dad bought it in Paris. She said he told her he saved up six months so he could get it for her." Billy sighed softly. "There was no doubt that they really loved each other. After she died, dad just wasn't the same. When Mom was alive, the three of us used to do fun things together. We went bowling and fishing, saw movies, all kinds of stuff, but afterward, that all stopped. I think it reminded him of her." Billy swallowed. If he didn't stop, he was going to become completely maudlin.

Looking in the box again, he saw some more papers in the bottom. "Finally," Billy breathed softly. "I was hoping we'd find these." Billy unfolded the papers and handed them to Darryl. "The boys' birth certificates."

Darryl set them on the table, and Billy looked them over. "Do these look okay to you?" He pulled out his and set them side by side.

"Sure, why?"

"I don't know. They just look different."

"Maybe because they're sixteen years newer."

"Probably." Billy folded up the certificates, placing them in his pocket. Then he put all the other papers and jewelry back in the box. "After lunch tomorrow, I need to take these down to the school."

"Not a problem." Darryl waited until Billy had everything packed up and followed Billy up the stairs, turning off the light. "Let's put that in a safe place and go to bed."

Billy agreed, and after putting the box on the shelf in his closet, he got undressed and joined Darryl under the covers. "I have everything I could want," he said softly, as much to himself as to Darryl, who hugged him close as he softly kissed his neck. But secretly, he wondered how long it could last.

CHAPTER NINE

"HEY, Billy, did you drop those papers off at the school?" Darryl asked, having remembered that Billy hadn't mentioned it.

"Yup," he smiled. "I just have to take them to the doctor to make sure that have all their immunizations, and they'll be all set to start kindergarten in the fall." Billy pulled open the back door of the restaurant, and the boys rushed into what they now considered their room without even looking around. The floor was littered with trucks, car, building blocks—you name it. Billy threaded through the mayhem to where the boys had already begun playing. "Tonight before we leave, you need to make sure all the toys are put away."

"Okay, Biwwy," they responded without looking up.

"I mean it. You wouldn't want Uncle Darryl to trip on anything and hurt himself when he has to do his book work?"

They both stopped playing. Guilt—it was a wonderful thing sometimes. "We'll clean up." As if to demonstrate, they began picking up the blocks and putting them in their bag. Billy noticed they got about half of them picked up before losing interest and returning to their trucks.

"I'll be in to check on you later, and the toys better be picked up."

"We will."

Billy knew the battle wasn't over but figured he'd fight it later, when he had the big guns available. Over the last week or so, he'd discovered that they tended to do what Darryl wanted when he asked, and they'd try to weasel out of things with Billy. It didn't work, but they still tried. Closing the lower half of the Dutch door, a recent addition, Billy walked through the kitchen, sharing a smile with Darryl as he passed before entering the dining room and starting work.

The lunch rush was particularly busy, and Billy barely got a chance to check on the boys for more than a second. As lunch wound down, Billy got a few minutes to go back. Peering over the door, he saw Davey watching television while Donnie slept curled up next to him on the futon, and not a toy had been picked up. In fact, more had been dragged out. The floor looked like a toy minefield. "Davey," he said quietly, "turn off the television and start picking up the toys." It must have been the stern look on his face, because the little boy slid off the futon and walked to the TV, pressing the power button.

"What about Donnie?" He turned and pointed at his sleeping brother.

"If you pick up the toys, then you get to choose the stories tonight at bedtime."

Davey's eyes widened, and he began picking up the trucks, placing them in the box in the corner. Smiling to himself, Billy went back through the kitchen to the dining room.

"Hey, Billy, there's a lady to see you." Sebastian pointed to a woman sitting in one of the booths. "She asked for you by your full name," Sebastian added ominously.

Wondering what she could want, Billy walked over, wiping his hands on a towel. "I'm Billy Weaver."

The woman stood up. "My name is Helen Groveson, with Cumberland County Child Services, and I have a few questions that I need to ask you about"—she opened her bag and pulled out a small notebook—"David and Donald Weaver."

"My brothers."

"Yes." She suddenly looked uncomfortable. "Is there a place we can talk privately?"

"Other than the booth in the far corner, I'm afraid not." Billy looked around and then back at her, wondering what in the hell was going on.

She shrugged. "I suppose it'll have to do." And she picked up her bag, following Billy to the booth.

"Would you like a cup of coffee?" Billy asked nervously.

"No, thank you." She motioned toward the other seat, and he slid into the booth. "I want you to know that we were called by the school due to an irregularity in Donald and David's enrollment application. It's standard for them to call us, and most of the time, it turns out to be nothing, but we have to investigate." Billy nodded, watching her face for some sort of clue as to what this was all about. "Can you tell me how long you've been taking care of your brothers?"

"My father died a few months ago, and I've been caring for them full time since then. Before that, I'd been watching out for them almost since they were born. My mother died a few weeks after their birth, and I'm sad to say that her death hit my father pretty hard."

"It must have been difficult taking care of them at such a young age." Some of the hard edge to her expression faded.

"I love them," Billy replied simply, as though that explained everything.

She consulted her notes. "The boys were born at Christian General Hospital outside Richmond, Virginia."

"Yes. We were living outside Richmond at the time the boys were born. Mom had been having a difficult time for a while. I remember my dad being very worried about her. But she had the babies, and they came home a few days later. From what I remember, she was doing okay for about a week, and then Dad took her to the hospital again in a big hurry, leaving me to watch the boys." Billy wiped his eyes with his sleeve. "She never came home again." He sniffled and straightened himself up. "She died a few days later." Billy got up and grabbed a napkin from the server's station and returned to the booth, wiping his eyes.

"Did your father ever behave strangely?"

Billy furrowed his brow. "I don't know how to answer that question. After my mother died, he wasn't the same. He drank more often than he should and couldn't seem to hold down a job for very long. I think we moved at least two times a year since then, and unfortunately, each time was to a place worse and worse."

"Did he treat David and Donald well?"

"I guess. As the years went by and I got older, I began taking care of them more and more. I think they reminded him of her so much that he just couldn't take it. When he died, they said his heart gave out, but I think it was just broken and he didn't want to go on any more." Billy wiped his eyes one last time and shoved the napkin in his pocket. "Can you tell me what this is about?"

"I can." She seemed to become uncomfortable, and Billy waited. He'd been uncomfortable since he'd started talking to her. "Is there someone close to you who can be with you?" She swallowed hard.

"Would you like a glass of water?"

Her gaze, which had shifted around the room, shifted back to him. "Yes, please."

Billy got up and went to the server station, getting a glass of ice water and setting it on the table before walking into the kitchen.

"What's wrong?" Darryl rushed around the counter to him as soon as he saw Billy's face.

"There's a woman out front from Child Services asking questions about the boys." Billy found himself starting to shake. "I asked her what this was all about, and she asked if there was someone who could be with me." Billy fought back tears as he felt Darryl's arms around him, holding him tight.

"It'll be okay, Billy. I promise you, it'll be fine." Darryl stroked his hair and held him. "Let's go see what she has to say before we get too upset, okay?" He felt Darryl's finger under his chin. "Whatever she wants, I'll help you any way I can. You know that."

"I do." Billy felt the knot in his stomach loosen somewhat, and he let Darryl lead him out front to the booth where Helen was waiting for them. "This is Darryl, he's the owner of the restaurant…."

Darryl held out his hand. "I'm Billy's partner." They shook, and Billy slid into the booth. Darryl sat right next to him, their hands clasped. "Would you please tell us what this is all about? Those boys have been through a lot lately, and we won't have their lives interrupted without a good reason." Billy thought Darryl was being a little gruff, but he said nothing, and Helen didn't seem to flinch at all. He figured she'd probably seen everything in her job and nothing fazed her.

"As I told Mr. Weaver, the school called us about an anomaly with David and Donald's application for school." Her voice seemed to soften. "Look, I'm doing my job, and sometimes I don't particularly like it. Well, today is one of those days." By the end of her thought, she'd gotten almost quiet. "The school thought something wasn't quite right with the boys' birth certificates and called the county where they were born. According to their records, David and Donald Weaver died a day after birth five years ago."

Billy felt his mouth hang open, and he could barely breathe. "What the hell are you talking about, lady? They're here with us." He could feel his temper starting to swell, and Darryl patted his hand gently.

"What is it you're saying?"

"There may have been a mix-up. It's been known to happen, but they're rare. We've been investigating, and we believe, and your story backs up our theory, that David and Donald died at birth and your father took another set of twins from the hospital, switching them for his dead children."

"That's nuts. My father could never have done that!" Billy struggled to get out of the booth, and Darryl did his best to calm him.

"Mr. Weaver, we don't know for sure, but the boys' birth certificates appear to have been altered, and you said yourself that shortly after your mother's death, your father started moving regularly."

Billy felt his anger slip away as complete and total abject fear took its place. "Are you saying that my brothers, the boys I've raised since they were brought home, aren't really my brothers?"

"We don't know, Mr. Weaver, but there is ample evidence. I came here today to tell you what we suspected and to ask you if you would be willing to submit to a DNA sample. We'd need one from the boys as well."

Billy shook his head. He could feel his mind shutting down. This couldn't be happening, there was just no way. Closing his eyes, he tried to block it out, hoping he'd wake up from this nightmare. When he opened them again, that awful woman was still there, and this hell wasn't a sick dream.

"Mr. Weaver, we could get a court order for DNA samples, and at the same time, we'd petition for the county to take temporary custody of the boys. Neither of us wants that." She turned to Darryl. "As you've said, those boys have been through enough, and if we're right, they'll go through a lot more. But if we're wrong, then they don't have to know, and they can happily go on with their lives."

"This is too much." Billy let his head fall forward, resting it on the table.

"I know this is hard, Mr. Weaver, but I want to ask you this. You aren't the only person involved in this. If these children aren't your brothers...."

"They are my brothers no matter what," Billy ground out between clenched teeth.

"Mr. Weaver, if the boys aren't your blood brothers," she amended carefully, "then there's someone out there who's missing their children."

Billy felt as though he'd been punched and kicked at the same time, and this last was the worst blow. "We'll submit to a DNA test if just to prove that Davey and Donnie are my brothers and that you're full of shit."

Helen got up. "I'll make the arrangements and be in contact." She took a step from the table and stopped. "And for the record, I sincerely hope that I am full of shit on this one."

Strangely, Billy realized that she was being truthful, and that made him feel a little better, but not freakin' much.

"Let's get you home." He heard Darryl's voice in his ear, but it barely registered.

Darryl slid out of the booth, and Billy managed to get to his feet, walking in a bit of a daze through the kitchen to where the boys were playing. "Hi, Biwwy," Davey called, all grinning teeth. "See, I picked up all the toys!" He had, too. The box in the corner was bursting and wouldn't close, but all the toys were off the floor. Granted, as soon as either of them got another one, the floor would be littered with the toys that spilled out of the box, but that didn't matter. Davey looked so proud of himself. "I get to choose the story."

Donnie rubbed his eyes as he slid off the futon, walking to the toy box and yanking out his truck.

"Donnie, pick those up." Davey had his hands on his hips in full five-year-old indignation.

Billy started to laugh, but he was soon choked with tears that wouldn't stop. Try as he might, they kept coming. Turning away so the boys wouldn't see, he made for the bathroom and shut the door, holding the sink as he was wracked with spasms. No sound came out, and all the air rushed from his lungs. Finally, he managed to take a gasping breath and let out a cry that filled the tiny room. He felt his legs buckle from beneath him, and he collapsed onto the floor.

He didn't hear the door open and close. All he felt were Darryl's arms around him, holding him tightly as he was rocked back and forth. Holding Darryl around the neck, Billy buried his head against his lover's shoulder and sobbed uncontrollably. If what she had said was true, Billy didn't know how he could possibly go on. All the grief over his father, old grief about his mother, joined with the fear and loss of possibly losing Davey and Donnie, too, was just too much. He felt both his mind and body shut down. The only thing he was aware of at all was Darryl.

"It's okay, love. Let it out." Darryl's soothing tone cut through his own grief. "You're allowed to cry, so you just go right ahead."

Billy held on to Darryl for dear life, like without him, he was going to be lost and would never find himself again. "They are my brothers. No matter what she says, they are my brothers."

"And no one can take that away from you. No matter what, they are your brothers, and you'll always love them, and they'll always love you. No matter what," Darryl soothed as he continued slowly rocking him. "But you need to be strong for them. They need you."

Slowly, Darryl's words sank in, and the grief subsided. Billy lifted his face away from Darryl's wet shirt and looked around. "How did I get in here?" He had no memory at all of getting to the bathroom. Darryl helped him to his feet, and Billy turned on the water, splashing some on his face before taking a deep breath.

"I think we need to get you home."

Billy shook his head. "I'll be okay. The boys need everything to be as normal as possible, and Sebastian is off tonight." Billy wiped his eyes with a paper towel. "He has a date, and I can't let him down."

"Are you going to be in any shape to work this evening?" Darryl's voice held only concern.

"I will be." Billy gave Darryl another hug before washing his hands and opening the bathroom door to half the staff standing in the hallway.

"What...?"

"Are you okay?" Sebastian had obviously been elected spokesman for the group.

"Thank you. Yes." Billy made his way through the group and into where the boys were playing, unaware that anything had happened. Sitting on the floor with them, he picked up a truck and started running it along the floor. The boys did the same, and soon the room was filled with "vroom, vroom" sounds. Billy tried to hold himself together as his mind captured everything as if it were precious. A part of his mind refused to believe what Helen said might be true, and another part wanted to hold on to everything in case it was the last time. A tear threatened, but Billy fought it back and kept playing. They spent the afternoon running the trucks. With his help, they built a tower out of cardboard blocks that reached from the floor to the ceiling. One of the boys would knock it down, and they'd build it again so the other one could take his turn.

"You guys having fun?" Darryl poked his head over the half door.

"Come play with us," Donnie called, and Darryl opened the door and stepped inside, joining them in their quest to build a bigger, taller tower.

CHAPTER TEN

DARRYL felt Billy roll over in bed for the millionth time that night. "You haven't slept at all, have you?"

"No." Billy continued staring at the ceiling, and Darryl pulled him closer, knowing he needed to know that he was there. "I keep thinking about what I'm going to do." He rolled onto his side. "What if they aren't Mom and Dad's children?" Darryl noticed that Billy didn't ask, "What if they're not my brothers?" because he knew in Billy's mind they were his brothers and always would be. "What if someone comes and takes them away?"

"Then we'll fight it with everything we've got." Darryl held his terrified lover close. "You raised those boys for the last five years, and they are your brothers. We're not going to allow anyone to just rip them away from you."

He felt but didn't hear Billy start to cry. "I spent half the night thinking that maybe I should take the boys and run."

"I know you don't really mean that. You love those boys too much to do that to them." Daryl didn't add that he hoped Billy loved him too much to leave like that, but he just couldn't bring himself to say it.

"I know. I couldn't do it to them, or to you. I just love them so much." The tears started again in earnest, and Darryl held his young lover, rocking him again as he cried. Darryl knew that before this whole thing played out, there would be plenty more tears to come.

Darryl held Billy, and he thought he might have dozed off for a little while. Eventually they both gave up and got out of bed. They dressed in silence, Darryl watching Billy's slow movements, his mind definitely somewhere else. "The people from the health department will be here soon. I got them to come early. They weren't happy about it, but I really don't care."

Billy nodded his head absently, and Darryl wasn't even sure he'd been heard, but he wasn't too worried about it. He'd help him however he could. After dressing, they got the boys up and dressed and gave them breakfast. When they were done eating, Billy wandered off with the boys to wait for the executioners.

A knock at the front door told Darryl that they'd arrived. Giving Billy's shoulder a squeeze, he walked through the house and opened the door. A man and a woman stood on the front step, both trying to suppress a yawn. "We're with the health department." They both showed their official identification. "I'm Gerald Forrester, and this is Margaret Jessup. We're here to take DNA samples from—" He consulted his sheet. "—William, David, and Donald Weaver."

"Yes." Darryl stepped back so they could enter and closed the door behind them. "They're in the living room." He motioned them through and followed them in.

Billy sat on the sofa with one of the boys on either side of him, an arm around each of them protectively. He looked as though he was ready to bolt at any second. Introductions were made, and the people got down to work. "What we're going to do is swab the inside of each of your cheeks." Ms. Jessup took out what looked like a big Q-tip and showed it to all three of them. "I need to do four from each of you, and then we'll be done." She smiled, and Darryl saw both Davey and Donnie shrink back into the sofa.

"You can do me first," Billy said, trying to reassure the kids.

She took out four swabs, each in a sterilized package, and four sealed containers. After writing all kinds of information on the containers, she slipped on rubber gloves and opened the package for the first swab. "Open your mouth wide."

Darryl watched as she twisted the swab around inside Billy's mouth, removed it, and then put it into one of the containers. Then she repeated the process three more times, sealing each of the containers and putting them in a case.

Taking off her gloves, she smiled at the boys. "Which of you wants to be first?"

"Me." Davey sat forward and opened his mouth, tilting his head back, looking like a baby bird. Darryl laughed and joined the others in the room, sitting next to Donnie and holding the little boy's hand. Donnie looked up at him and tried to smile. In that instant, Darryl realized Donnie knew something was very wrong and felt him burrow next to him like he was trying to hide behind him.

"You were very good." She finished swabbing Davey's mouth and turned to Donnie. "Are you ready?" She smiled at him.

"No," Donnie gritted out, keeping his mouth closed before putting his hands over his face and turning away.

"It won't hurt, Donnie, I promise," Darryl said, but he could see the fear in his eyes. The kid might not know what exactly was happening, but he knew something was wrong, and he was determined not to cooperate. "Will you do it for me?" Darryl asked, and Donnie's hands slipped away from his face. "Thank you." Darryl turned to Margaret. "You're only going to get one shot at this."

"I understand." She smiled at Donnie and gave him one of the swabs, taking it out of the wrapper and handing it to him so he could see it. He played with it and handed it to Darryl, who looked at it and handed it back. When she was ready, she turned to Donnie. "Would you open your mouth like a big boy?"

Donnie complied, and she swabbed one after the other. As soon as she was done, he snapped his little mouth closed and made icky faces, again burying his head against Darryl.

"Thank you." She reached into her bag and pulled out a lollipop and handed one to each of the boys. Davey took his and immediately opened it, shoving it into his mouth, while Donnie just held his and stared at it.

"What do you say?" Billy prompted.

"Fank you!" Davey replied, his mouth full.

Donnie mouthed something softly and then climbed onto Darryl's lap, holding to him tightly.

"You're welcome." She got her things together, and the two of them walked toward the door. Darryl handed Donnie to Billy and followed them outside.

"How long will it take until we hear the results?"

"It should be about a week to ten days. Half the swabs are being sent to Virginia, and half will be tested here. I know this sounds cliché, but the waiting is the hardest part."

"If you decide you need someone to talk to," Gerald said, and handed him a card, "please feel free to give me a call. The waiting and not knowing can be very hard, and sometimes it helps to talk."

Darryl took the card and shook both of their hands, watching as they drove away before going back inside.

He found Billy still sitting on the sofa, the boys having wandered off. "You going to be okay?" He rubbed Billy's shoulders and leaned over the back of the sofa, kissing his ear. "I know this is hard, and I'm here for you."

"I know." Billy turned around, and Darryl saw a fleeting glance of the pain Billy was feeling. "It's not just losing the boys."

Darryl let go and walked around the sofa, sitting next to his lover. "What is it?"

"It's sort of weird." Billy stopped, and Darryl took his hand and waited as patiently as he could. "But I sort of feel as though I don't know who I am." Billy shifted on the sofa so they could see each other. "My dad might have stolen two children to pass off as his own. What kind of person does that? I just feel like the family I thought I had wasn't real."

Darryl sat quietly, but Billy had said what he wanted to, his eyes closing. "It was real. Those boys are real, and the way you feel about them is real. I don't think anything else matters."

"What am I going to do, Darryl?" It looked as though Billy was going to break down again, but he didn't. Darryl watched as his back straightened and his eyes blinked rapidly.

"They said it'll take a week to ten days before we hear anything. I think we need to make the most of the time we have and prepare for either answer."

"You mean prepare for the worst, don't you?" Billy jumped to his feet and began pacing the floor. "I refuse to give up hope, Darryl. I won't turn my back on what I know in my heart."

"I'm not asking you to." Darryl almost stood up, but he figured Billy didn't want his comfort right now. "We'll deal with whatever comes up, but we both have to accept the possibility that what Helen said is true. I sure as hell hope she's wrong, but what if she's not? What if Davey and Donnie aren't related to you? Are you going to be able to handle that?" He tried to keep his voice level and calm, but he wasn't managing very well, he knew that. Reaching out, he touched Billy's hand. "I know I'm not helping you very much, but I just want you to be okay."

"What about the boys? Will they be okay if they suddenly find out that they're going to live with complete strangers? What if they won't let me see them again?" Billy began to shake, and Darryl had had enough.

Getting up, he pulled Billy to him. "Sometimes I forget just how young you are." He felt Billy tense, but Darryl didn't let him go, and slowly some of the tension slipped out of him, and then Billy returned the hug. "This is a lot for anyone to bear."

"I'm not a child, Darryl. I raised my brothers and saw that they had a place to live and fed them… somehow."

"Billy, you are stronger than most people I know. No matter what happens, you'll make it through this. I know your imagination is conjuring up the worst right now, so try to concentrate on the here and now. The only way you'll get through this is to take it one day at a time."

"I know you're right. And I can't let this affect the boys." Billy rested his head against Darryl's shoulder. "So, what do we do?"

"We have to go on." Over Billy's shoulder, he checked his watch. "And we need to get to work, or we'll never be ready for lunch."

"I know." Billy let him go, sighing softly. "I need to get the boys ready, and then we can leave."

They made it to the restaurant, and Billy got the boys settled. Since they were running late, Darryl had to get right to work.

"You getting enough sleep?" Maureen asked as she worked.

"No." Darryl looked around before giving her the shortened version of what was happening. "I don't want this to get around. He's upset enough as it is."

"God," was Maureen's only reply. "I can't imagine how he feels. I mean, if someone tried to take my kids away from me, I'd claw their eyes out, and that was after I twisted their gonads off." She made a motion with her hands that had Darryl crossing his legs. "Do you think it's possible that Davey and Donnie aren't his brothers?"

"I'm afraid it's a distinct possibility." He felt as though he was betraying Billy even voicing the thought. Before he could say anything else, he heard footsteps and clammed up. Billy walked past and gave him a smile that didn't hide an ounce of the misery he was feeling. "I wish there was something I could do to help him."

"All you can do is be there for him. And I'll let you in on a secret: when I was about to give birth, I called Eric every name in the book and some that hadn't been thought of yet. I blamed him for the pain and told him he was responsible for everything from global warming to the Arab-Israeli conflict."

Darryl looked at her, thinking the woman had completely lost her mind. But Maureen just smiled at him.

"Billy's under a lot of stress, and it's not going to end until he has an answer. If it's a good one, then he'll deal with it and move on. But if it's not, then the stress will only continue to build, and you're the one that'll take the brunt of it. So don't be surprised if he blames you for everything and even takes it out on you a little. It doesn't mean he doesn't love you, it just means he doesn't quite know how to cope with it."

Darryl smiled as though she was kidding.

"I'm serious," Maureen added.

Darryl nodded slowly, letting her message sink in. "Did you really blame Eric for global warming?"

"Uh-huh, I told him everything bad in the world was the fault of men and that global warming was all caused by men breathing hot air. Thankfully he just shook his head indulgently and asked the doctor to give me more drugs. The man was a genius."

"I don't think I'll have that luxury with Billy." Darryl went back to finishing his preparations as he heard Kelly come into the kitchen.

"No, but it was his love that got us through—that and some great chemicals. You'll get him through as well. I guess I'm saying you'll need patience and a lot of understanding."

The door to the dining room swung open. "I'm unlocking the doors, and as a heads-up, there's a large group of ladies outside, so we're going to be busy right away."

"How's Billy?" Darryl asked softly.

Sebastian peeked out and let the door close behind him. "He's told me what's happening, and he's holding together well for now." Sebastian stepped a little closer. "I'll keep an eye on him."

"Thanks."

"No sweat." Sebastian left the kitchen. Soon the orders began coming in, and they were slammed for the next few hours. Whenever he had a short break between orders, Darryl looked in on the boys. He actually found himself leaning against the door watching them play. At one point, Kelly touched him on the back and pointed to the orders lining the board, and he forced himself back to work. "Fuck—Billy's not the only one who could get hurt," he muttered to himself as he got back to work and started filling the orders.

The lunch service finally finished, and Darryl heard his name being called. Walking back, he found both boys jumping up to see over the door. They knew they were to stay inside unless they had to go to the bathroom. "We're hungry."

"Didn't you eat lunch?" he asked, and they both nodded their heads.

"We want ice cream."

Darryl opened the door and held out his hands. Each boy took one, and he led them to the dining room. The customers were gone, and the staff was working to clean up and prepare for later in the day. "Anybody want ice cream?" All work stopped. He showed the boys to a booth and told them to stay there and he'd bring them some ice cream in a minute.

By the time he got back with ice cream, bowls, and a scoop, everyone had gathered around and the boys had their spoons out, chattering away as they banged on the table. Dishing up two small bowls, he passed them to the boys and then began dishing out for everyone else. They worked hard, and everyone deserved a treat. But he didn't see Billy.

Looking around the room, he saw his lover behind the bar, washing glasses and cleaning up. Walking around, he came up behind him. "Don't you want some ice cream?" Billy shook his head. "The boys are wondering where you are."

"I know, but I just can't watch them being all happy, knowing what's hanging over us. I'll just start to blubber." Billy rinsed the cloth he was using to wipe out the refrigerator into his pan and wrung it out before attacking the shelves again. "I know I sound stupid." He finished what he was doing and put the cloth in the water and closed the door. "But I just need to keep busy."

Darryl knelt down next to him. "Baby, you can't run away from this, and you can't ignore them for a week because it hurts. I know it doesn't compare, but it hurts for me, too, and I just want to spend every second with them. If I could, I'd close the restaurant and we'd spend every day doing fun things, just the four of us. But I can't."

"Okay, you're right." Billy stood up and lifted the pan of dirty water, pouring it down the drain and turning on the tap. "Let's have some ice cream."

The others had nearly finished, putting their bowls in the dish room and returning to work. Both Darryl and Billy slid into the booth, and Donnie offered Billy his spoon filled with ice cream. Billy took the offered bite and smiled at his brother, hugging the little boy closer.

"Sometimes there's something to be said for the simple things in life," Billy commented as he accepted another bite from Donnie with a smile.

Darryl could see that while his mouth was smiling, Billy's eyes held worry. Thinking about it, he realized he felt the same worry and fear, except in his case, it wasn't just for Davey and Donnie, but for Billy as well.

"Can we go to the park?" Davey asked, waving around his empty spoon, and Darryl had to duck to escape the weapon-wielding five-year-old.

"Darryl and I have to work," Billy said as he gathered up the empty bowls. "But we'll go this weekend, I promise." The boys seemed content and raced through the kitchen doors. Darryl hoped the test results didn't come back too fast and that they'd be able to fulfill Billy's promise. Hell, what he really hoped was that they'd be able to fulfill that promise every Sunday until the boys learned to drive.

CHAPTER ELEVEN

TEN days. The last ten days had been like spending a month in the fires of hell for Billy. Every time the phone rang, he jumped a mile. A few days ago, he had answered the phone to discover it was Darryl's mother. When he'd told her that he'd get Darryl, she'd explained that she wanted to speak with him. It seemed that Darryl had told her the story of what was happening, and she'd called to offer her support. "You and those twins make my son happy." Billy could tell that Cordy Hansen was a lioness when it came to anyone who threatened her family. "I always thought he'd spend his life alone, working in a restaurant until the day he died, but he thinks the world of you."

"Thank you. I love your son." Why he told her that he didn't know, but it just flew out of his mouth.

"I know you do, and if there's anything you need, like a lawyer or even just to talk, we're here."

"Okay, thanks." Billy hadn't known what to make of the conversation and had handed the phone to Darryl, who talked for a few minutes before saying goodbye. "Is your mom for real?"

"Yes. I think she figures you're some kind of superman or something. She told me they're coming for a visit later this summer and that she and my dad are both looking forward to meeting you."

Billy had shaken his head in wonder, smiling as he tried to imagine what Darryl's parents were like.

The phone ringing pulled him out of his thoughts, and Billy tried his best to tamp down the twist in his stomach. The ringing stopped, and he heard Darryl's voice drift into the room. Then Darryl walked into the room and sat down in the chair next to him. "That was Helen Groveson. They have the results of the tests, and she asked if she could come over. I told her we were home, and she said she'd be here in a few minutes."

Billy swallowed his coffee, trying to keep himself from panicking. "Did she say anything?"

"No." Darryl sighed and took his hand. Billy returned his grip and tried to settle down his nerves, but it wasn't working.

"Excuse me." Billy raced for the bathroom and managed to reach it before the little he'd had for breakfast came right back up.

"It'll be okay." He felt Darryl's hand on his back, rubbing softly as he reached for a tissue to wipe his mouth. "I know I've said it before, but whatever happens, we'll deal with it together."

Billy straightened up and flushed. "I know. It's just that...." Billy couldn't finish his thought as he squeezed his eyes closed and felt his shoulders shake. "Whoever these people are, what if they hurt them?"

"We don't know the results yet."

Billy knew Darryl was trying to soothe him and help him feel better, but he was having none of it. A knock on the door echoed through the house, and Billy suddenly stopped moving, standing stark still. "Go ahead, I'll be along in a minute."

He felt Darryl give him a fast hug, and then he was alone. Closing the door, he stood in front of the mirror and looked at himself, dabbing his eyes and doing his best to make himself look presentable. But it wasn't working. "Don't be such a girl." Shaking his head and taking a deep breath, he wiped his eyes again and opened the door, following the sound of voices into the living room.

Helen stood up and extended her hand. Billy shook it and then sat down next to Darryl, who threaded his arm around his waist. "Can you tell me where the boys are?"

"In the backyard, playing with the fish," Billy commented dryly. "They've named them and keep trying to catch them, but Gordon and Anna are too fast for them." Billy stopped talking and waited for her to say what she had to say.

"The tests came back, and I'm very sad to tell you that David and Donald are not your parents' children. They are the biological children of Marie and Charles Hanover. The tests positively confirmed it on all fronts." Billy felt Darryl's arm tighten around him, holding him steady, but Billy heard nothing at all after that. His mind nearly stopped thinking, and if he could have willed it, his heart would have stopped as well.

"Billy." He heard Darryl say his name though what felt like a haze, and he refocused his eyes as Helen continued talking.

"As I was saying," she continued, her voice light and full of empathy. "The Hanovers have agreed to come to Carlisle, and they'll stay for about a week or so. They understand the boys know none of this and that they'll need some time to build a relationship with them before they take them home. I also made it clear to them when we spoke that you had nothing at all to do with them being taken and that you had raised them as though they were your own."

"Will I be able to see them?" Billy managed to croak out the words as his eyes filled with tears, and he buried his face in Darryl's shoulder, crying his heart out. He felt Darryl's hand on his back, and it took him a few minutes to get hold of himself again.

"That will be up to the Hanovers, but I have been involved in a few cases like this in my career, and I'll tell you that I will be pressing for visitation for you. It's in the best interest of the children. After all, biological or not, you are their brother." She stood up. "I'll leave you." She handed Darryl her card. "Please call me if there's anything I can do." Darryl got up, but Billy just couldn't bring himself to do it. He heard the door open and close but just sat where he was. When Darryl didn't come back right away, he waited.

Hearing the front door open and close again, he got up and walked through the house, finding Darryl on the phone. "Maureen, would you please call Julio and see if he can work lunch as well as dinner tonight?" Billy moved closer, and Darryl hugged him as he continued talking. "See if he's willing to work tomorrow as well. I don't think either of us is going to be up to anything. I'll call you later and let you know what's happening." Darryl hung up the phone and pulled him into a full-on hug.

"What else did Helen say?"

Darryl waited a few seconds before answering. "That the Hanovers would be traveling up here today and that she'd call us to arrange a place where we and the boys could meet them. They're not going to just pull the boys away. She also said that it would be best if we told the boys what was happening."

"How can I explain to them that their life up to now has all been a lie?" Billy felt himself start to cry again. This was overwhelming.

"Billy!" Darryl's voice held a rough edge. "You have to be strong—if not for yourself, then for them." Darryl pointed toward the back of the house. "They're going to be confused and will not understand what's happening. You are the only one who can help them through what is going to be a very difficult process. I know you love them, and because you do, you have to help them. Otherwise they'll be completely lost and confused."

"I know, Darryl." Billy clamped his eyes closed, trying to get himself under control. "Let's go see what they're up to." Billy started walking toward the back.

The boys were running their trucks all over the paved yard. The flower beds looked the worse for wear, but neither Billy nor

Darryl minded. "Guys, could you come inside for a while? There's something I need to tell you." The steadiness in Billy's voice surprised him, and he wiped his eyes and ushered the boys into the living room. He had no idea how to tell them what he needed to or how much they would or could understand, but he knew he had to do it.

Billy sat on the floor with the boys sitting in front of him, Darryl sitting next to him. "This is very hard for me to tell you, and I just found out today." He took a deep breath and looked into their big, inquisitive eyes. Neither of them moved or squirmed the way they usually did. "When you were born, your daddy took you from the hospital, but you weren't his babies. Your real mommy and daddy were someone else, and they've been looking for you for a long time." Billy stopped, not knowing where he should go from here.

"Does this mean you aren't our brother no more?" Davey stood up and rushed to him, throwing himself at Billy and hugging him hard, with Donnie right behind him.

"No, I'll always be your brother, no matter what." He returned their hugs, holding them tight, like he never wanted to let them go. "But it does mean that your real mommy and daddy will be coming tomorrow to see you, and after awhile they'll take you home to live with them." Billy felt his heart rip to shreds as he said those words. In his mind, he knew that Davey and Donnie were his brothers, not his children, and that he would have normally left the house and made his own life by now. But these weren't normal circumstances. The three of them had been each other's family for months now, and even when his dad was alive, it had been the boys that Billy had lived for.

Donnie pulled away from Billy, crossing his hands over his chest. "I don't want to live anyplace else!" He stomped his feet and then ran out of the room and up the stairs.

"I'll stay with him," Darryl said as he left the room, and Billy heard his footsteps on the stairs.

"I don't want to leave either." Davey held tight around Billy's neck, and Billy stroked his little back as he cried against his Billy's shoulder. Billy felt his own tears threatening hard, but he shoved them back. He had to stay strong for them. "What if they're mean?"

"They won't be mean." That Billy seemed to know. Any couple who could produce children like his brothers couldn't have a mean bone in their body. That much Billy was sure of. "I'm sure they'll be nice people who will love both of you very much."

"As much as you?" Davey asked through his tears.

"Nobody will love you as much as I do." Billy hugged the little body to him and let his own tears fall. He couldn't hold them back any longer.

Footsteps on the stairs caught his attention. Turning around, he saw Darryl carrying and soothing a crying Donnie, the little boy's head on his shoulder. As all their tears settled down, Billy tried to talk again. "We'll answer any questions, we promise."

Davey, always the most forward of the two, spoke up. "If we have to leave, will you come visit?"

"Yes, of course I'll come visit you, and so will Uncle Darryl." Billy felt the tears try to start again, but he kept himself together through some miracle.

Donnie lifted his head off Darryl's shoulder. "Can we come here to visit sometimes?"

"Of course," Billy replied, and Davey began squirming. Billy let him go. "We'll be going to see them tomorrow morning."

"What if we don't like them?" Donnie asked quietly.

"Yeah," Davey echoed. "If I don't like them, then I'm coming back here." With that pronouncement, Davey walked out of the room and stomped up the stairs. As Billy expected, Donnie followed behind him, leaving Billy still sitting on the floor.

Darryl joined him, and he felt strong arms wrap around him. "I hope they'll be okay."

"They will, Billy, and so will you. I don't know anyone who could have handled that any better." The sound of a truck falling down the stairs made them both jump, and as it reached the landing, they saw Davey scrambling behind it, picking it up and flying back up that stairs. "We should see what they're up to."

Billy nodded and lifted himself up, following Darryl up the stairs. As they approached the door, he didn't hear anything. Pushing it open slightly, he saw both boys on the floor of their room, coloring pictures. "You make yours for Uncle Dawwyl, I'm making one for Biwwy, okay?" Davey instructed, and Donnie nodded his agreement before returning to his work.

He closed the door slowly and quietly walked back down the stairs. Turning around, he noticed Darryl rubbing his eyes. "This was a hard day."

"I know." Darryl went into the kitchen, and Billy heard the sound of pots and pans banging louder than they usually did.

"You can go into the restaurant if you need to. I'll stay here with the boys."

Darryl shook his head hard. "I'm staying; you need me a lot more than the restaurant does right now."

"I'm going to be okay," Billy said softly.

"I know you are, and so will the boys. They're your brothers, and no matter where they live, they'll always be your brothers." Darryl sighed and then went quiet as he began his cooking.

"What is it?"

"Nothing. It's kind of stupid," Darryl answered. Then he went on anyway. "I was just thinking how quiet the house will be without them. Before I met you, this house was kind of lifeless. You and the boys helped make it a home."

Billy didn't know how to respond to that. Darryl's house did feel like home—he just wasn't sure how it was going to feel once the boys were gone. God, he hated that thought, but there was no use denying it. He couldn't stop it, and he wasn't going to be selfish and make this harder on them than it already was. Opening the back door, he walked outside, the warmth and sunshine brightening his spirits a little. Looking around, he let himself smile a little as he picked up the toys and set them out of the way.

When lunch was ready, Darryl came out, followed by the boys, each carrying a picture they'd drawn. Davey jumped on Billy's lap and handed him the paper. "This is you," he pointed proudly. "This is Uncle Dawwyl, and this is Donnie and me." Their family.

Billy hugged him tight and listened as Donnie explained his picture. "This is Gordon and Anna."

"It looks like they're in your racecar bed," Darryl commented quizzically.

Donnie laughed. "They are," he answered matter-of-factly, as though fish belonged in racecar beds.

Darryl hugged him tightly and took the picture. "I'm going to put both of these on the refrigerator of fame." Hugs were shared all around, and Darryl brought out lunch. The boys sat at the outdoor table and ate with their usual vigor, while Billy just picked at his food, eating very little and tasting even less.

They spent the afternoon playing games together, and Billy found that he could get into it and allowed himself to have fun. It still felt like the last day of summer vacation, but he forced himself to try, and after a while, the hurt didn't matter so much. If the boys could run and play, so could he.

After dinner, they all went upstairs, and after bath time, Billy and Darryl took turn reading stories until the boys fell asleep, holding their stuffed toys tight. Closing their door, Billy went to the room he shared with Darryl and sat on the edge of the bed.

He heard Darryl come in but didn't look up. "I don't know what to do with myself."

He felt Darryl lifting him to his feet and went along with it, not having enough strength to fight him. His clothes were opened and slipped off his body, and he saw, through unfocused eyes, that Darryl was doing the same. "Lay back on the bed, love." Billy did as Darryl asked, and soon warm, magic hands danced over his skin. "I love you, Billy." He felt lips and a tongue follow those hands. "Turn off you mind and your worries. Just think of my hands and how they make you feel. Nothing else." Billy's forced himself to concentrate on Darryl's voice, and some of the tension slipped out of him. The bed felt softer and Darryl's hands felt warmer with every stroke. "Just relax and look at me."

Billy forced his eyes open and saw Darryl's eyes drilling into him, shining at him. "Love you, Darryl."

His lips were taken in a steaming kiss that helped drive other thoughts from his mind. "I love you too, Billy, my Billy." Hands kept stroking and lips kept kissing until Billy could barely remember his name, much less anything else. "I'm going to make love to you."

"Yes," Billy hissed through his teeth. "Love me, Darryl."

"I already do, I'm just going to show you how much."

"Yes."

All of Darryl's movements were slow and deliberate as Billy floated on clouds of sensation. All the worry and care seemed to float away as Darryl made love to him for the first time. The pain, the love, the loss, the sorrow, all blended together, banished by the love Darryl showed him. Billy's climax left him floating on air, and he didn't land until the following morning.

CHAPTER TWELVE

DARRYL paced the living room floor, waiting for Billy and the boys. If he was this nervous and jumpy, he knew Billy must be ready to jump out of his skin. All he wanted to do right now was jump into his car, rush to the restaurant, and cook. When he got really nervous or upset, he cooked—it was the one thing he knew could always calm his nerves. But today, that wasn't an option. Julio had called to tell him that everything had gone well the night before and that they had things in hand for today. "After all, I was trained by the best," Julio had quipped just before disconnecting.

Helen had called shortly afterward to tell them that the Hanovers were in town. They'd asked if they could meet them and the boys for lunch, but given the way emotions were running, Darryl had suggested they come to the house. "It'll be much better for the boys." Darryl had then gone on to explain the conversation they'd had with the boys and their reaction, and Helen agreed that the initial meeting should be held where Davey and Donnie felt most comfortable.

"Is that them?" Every noise had his lover jumpy.

"No." Darryl put an arm around his lover. If anything, he knew that the next week was going to be hardest on him. Darryl knew that Davey and Donnie would adjust, given time and plenty of love and attention. They were young and resilient, but Darryl knew that, in

Billy's mind, he was losing the last of his family. Both his mother and father were already dead, and now the brothers he'd thought he had weren't really his either. "Where are the boys?"

Billy rolled his eyes. "Where do you think?"

"Out back with the fish," Darryl deadpanned.

"You got it."

"Those have got to be the most traumatized fish on earth." Darryl felt Billy chuckle a little, and then the tension returned to his lover. "It's going to be okay." He'd said that a lot; he just hoped it was true.

Billy turned to look at him, his eyes surprisingly clear. "Is it wrong for me to hope they were in a fatal car accident?"

"Yes," Darryl replied, "but probably very natural." Darryl sat on the sofa and tugged Billy down with him, holding him. "I hope you realize how lucky Davey and Donnie are to have you." Billy didn't reply, so Darryl continued anyway. "How many people would care for their brothers the way you did? Even now, you're helping them."

"No, I'm not." Billy shook his head slowly.

"Yes, you are," Darryl reiterated. "Most people would get a lawyer and tie things up in the courts for years. Either that, or they'd run and try to hide somewhere. You're not doing that. Instead, you're helping them move on with their lives. Billy, you're helping them find their real parents. That's pretty amazing." The look in Billy's eyes told him at least some of what he was saying was getting through. "You're probably the most generous person I've ever met. I know you're hurting, and hurting badly, but you're still putting the boys above yourself, and that's pretty special."

"I love them and want them to be happy."

"I know." Darryl squeezed gently. "And I want you to be happy." What he really wished was that there was a way that everyone could be happy, but it just didn't look like that was completely possible. A knock on the door made them both jump slightly. "Are you ready?"

"As I'll ever be, I suppose." Billy stayed back as Darryl opened the front door.

Helen stood out front with a nervous-looking couple. Darryl took one look at them and any doubt that they were the boys' biological parents flew out the window. The boys were the spitting image their father. Their blue eyes, round face—he even had the same unruly cowlick in front that each of the boys had, even with his hair as short as it was. "Please come in." Darryl stepped back, and Helen led them inside.

"William, Darryl, this is Marie and Charles Hanover."

"Charlie, please," he corrected.

"Call me Billy." Darryl watched as they shook hands. "Please come into the living room."

"Can we see the boys?" Marie asked, obviously very nervous.

Helen took charge, to Darryl's relief. "I thought we should talk first. All of you have to have a million questions for each other. Darryl and Billy have explained to the boys what's happening, but they may be very shy and tentative. They will probably ask questions that one or all of you will find uncomfortable, but I can't stress enough that you need to be honest with them."

"We understand." Charles took his wife's had as he answered for them. "There is one thing I'd like to say. Marie and I realize that Billy didn't know what had happened and wasn't responsible for taking the twins from the hospital." Darryl saw Marie dab her eyes, and Charles did the same.

"Do you have other children?"

Marie shook her head. "I couldn't have any more after the twins." She fished into her purse for a handkerchief and blew her nose delicately before looking at both of them. "Do you know what happened at the hospital?"

"My father died a few months ago, and I only know what I've been told by Helen. Truthfully, I'm afraid many of the answers died with him." Billy's voice seemed surprisingly strong and clear.

"Where are the boys?" Marie asked, looking around the room.

"They're out back, playing. I'll bring them in." Billy got up and slowly left the room. Everyone sat quietly and waited. A few minutes later, Billy walked back in holding each of his brothers by the hand. As soon as they entered the room, Davey pulled his hand away and ran toward Darryl, jumping into his lap and holding him tight. "This is Donnie, and that's Davey. Say hello, boys."

Both of them looked at Marie and Charlie before turning away and hiding their faces.

"Donnie, that's no way to behave," Darryl scolded lightly.

"I don't wanna go anywhere, I wanna stay with Biwwy."

"Me too," Davey echoed without lifting his face from Billy's shoulder.

Darryl saw Marie flinch and reach for her handkerchief again. He knew he had to do something. "Would you like to show them Gordon and Anna?"

Donnie lifted his head for a second and thought about it before nodding slowly and looking at Marie and Charles, his eyes big.

"Then let's show them." Darryl stood up, still holding Donnie, and led the way through the house and out the back door. Putting Donnie down, he waited to see his reaction. Donnie walked up to the pond and pointed. Billy followed suit, and Davey joined him.

"Which one's Gordon?" Charlie asked.

"The yellow one," Davey answered, pointing. "The orange one is Anna." Both Charlie and Marie looked into the pond, watching the fish swim around.

"Do you both like trucks?" Charles asked as he looked at the toy-scattered patio. The boys nodded but didn't say anything, continuing to watch the fish. "Which one's your favorite?"

Davey was the first to take the bait, rushing over to the dump truck that Darryl had given him, pushing it around. The noise drew Donnie's attention, and he grabbed a steam shovel. Charlie knelt down and started running the bus around as well.

Davey wheeled his truck over. "That one takes kids to school," he explained to his father, and the smile on Charlie's face would have lit the night. Darryl stepped back and watched the conflicted look on Billy's face as Marie gingerly sat on the ground, pushing trucks across the pavement. "Billy," Darryl whispered, putting an arm around his waist, "we should go inside." The look on Billy's face told him that was the last thing he wanted to do, but he slowly nodded, and they stepped inside.

Helen followed them inside, and Darryl poured each of them a mug of coffee. "I feel as though I'm leaving my children with strangers," Billy commented softly as he sank into one of the dining room chairs.

"That's perfectly normal," Helen said as she wrapped her hands around the mug as though they were cold and sat across from him. Darryl sat next to Billy, holding his hand. "You're going to grieve their loss, and that's normal too." She raised the mug to her lips and sipped. "I spoke to them on the way over and explained that to the boys, you are their brother, and that they need to make sure that your relationship with Davey and Donnie has a chance to continue and flourish."

Billy stared at his mug without touching it. "I just can't figure out what I'm going to do without them."

"You were more than a brother to those boys, weren't you?"

Billy nodded but didn't answer, which had Darryl nervous again. As long as Billy was talking, he seemed okay, but when he got quiet, Darryl knew he was stewing again.

"You were more like a parent."

"Yeah, I guess I was." The "but I'm not anymore" that went unsaid hung in the room like a cloud.

"If I may make an observation, judging by how happy those boys are, you were a good parent. And one of the hardest things about having children is letting them go when the time comes. I had to do it when my son went off to college. Granted it's not at all the same thing here, but I think that's sort of what you're feeling." She took another sip. "All your time and effort has been wrapped up in those two."

Laughter filtered in from the yard, both from the boys and their parents. Darryl actually swallowed hard when the realization hit him—Charlie and Marie were Davey and Donnie's parents now.

"The thing is, you need to find your own life now. Build your relationship with Darryl, go back to school, whatever you want to do. The important thing is to find what makes you happy."

Billy sighed. "I wish I knew what that was." Billy tightened his grip on Darryl's hand. "Other than you." Billy rested his head his shoulder, and Darryl rubbed his lover's arm.

The sound of running in the house caught their attention as Davey rushed to Billy. "They play trucks good, Biwwy." He pulled on his arm. "Come play with us."

Darryl saw the yearning on Billy's face to do just that. "I'm going to talk with Helen for a while, but you go out and play. It sounds like you're having a lot of fun." Billy kept his voice level, even though Darryl knew that was very hard for him.

"Okay." Davey ran away and then returned. "Can we go to the park?"

"After lunch," Billy answered. Then he added, "Why don't you ask Marie and Charlie to come with us?"

Davey nodded vigorously as he rushed back outside to continue playing.

"I'm proud of you," Darryl said into Billy's ear.

Helen got up from the table. "I don't think I'm really needed right now, but you have my card, and I'll see you tomorrow."

Billy stood and shook her hand. "Thank you for everything." She said her goodbyes and then left the house.

"Come on." Darryl put their cups in the sink and then led Billy into the back room of the house and closed the door. "I think you deserve a little quiet time. I'm going to make lunch, and I'd like you to just relax for a while, if you want."

"Thank you." Billy looked like a wrung-out rag. The last two days had been exhausting for both of them, but especially for Billy. Darryl knew there were plenty of tears and goodbyes ahead, but Billy had taken the first step. "I love you, Darryl." Billy pulled him into a hug.

"I love you too. Very much." Darryl returned the hug. "This is the hardest thing anyone can go through, and you're handling it better than I would." The boys' laughter drifted in from the backyard.

Darryl saw the hurt flash on Billy's face. "They seem to be getting along."

"I know you secretly hoped they'd hate each other, but it's better for the boys that they do. Marie and Charlie are their legal parents now." Darryl heard Billy's soft groan. "But in their hearts, you will always be their brother, and it may hurt now, but you know you're doing what's right."

"I know, but it still hurts."

"Of course it does, and you're allowed to hurt. You're allowed to cry and be grouchy about it if you want—just not too grouchy." Darryl smirked, but Billy didn't react, and he let it slide. "Rest awhile. I'll make lunch and keep an eye on the boys."

"Thanks." Billy stepped away, and Darryl already missed his touch. Suppressing the urge to draw him back, he let Billy settle on the sofa and covered him with a light blanket. He hadn't slept well in days and was looking rather drawn, with circles beneath his eyes. Darryl really didn't expect Billy to sleep, but he hoped the man would at least rest a little. Besides, the boys needed to spend some time with their parents. They had to get to know them and build a relationship with them, and Darryl figured they wouldn't do that if Billy was always around.

Maybe he was wrong, and that nagged at him a little, but Darryl knew that in about a week, the boys would be leaving with Marie and Charlie, and it would be just him and Billy. Leaning over, he gave Billy a kiss before quietly leaving the room and going to the kitchen.

He'd just started when Marie stuck her head in. "Need any help?" she asked, her Virginia accent suddenly very pronounced.

"No, thank you. This kitchen's pretty small, but if you'd like to pull up a chair, I could use some company."

She brought one of the dining room chairs closer and sat in the doorway and started talking. "When we got the call that they'd found our boys, we weren't sure we could believe it. After all this time, I'm ashamed to say I figured they were prob'ly dead." She dabbed her eyes as she looked back into the house. "This has got to be one of the strangest situations I could ever have imagined."

Darryl had to smile. The situation was pretty amazing—crazy, and nearly downright bizarre. "Have they told you much about Billy and the boys?"

"Not really." She was watching him movements intently. "You sure know what yer doing."

Darryl explained about his restaurant, and then they talked food. Darryl even got her recipe for fried chicken. Every now and then, they'd hear laughter from outside. When lunch was ready, Darryl went to get Billy, and the six of them ate in the backyard. Davey and Donnie insisted on sitting on either side of Billy.

"Can we go to the park now?" Davey asked as he shoved the last of his food into his mouth.

"We'll go when the rest of us are done," Billy answered, and Davey sat in his chair fairly quietly. But Darryl could see his little mind running, trying to figure out how to make everyone eat faster.

Davey practically clapped for joy when the plates were cleared. He and Donnie raced into the house and up to their rooms, returning with their jackets on and racing to the kitchen. "Can we feed the ducks?"

"Sure." Darryl got a loaf of bread and divided it into bags, and the boys ran to the front door. "Why don't you two ride with Charlie and Marie?" Both boys looked at him strangely but nodded. Their momentary insecurity was quickly overcome by their excitement as they followed their new parents out the door, each carrying their half of the bread.

Locking the door, Darryl and Billy got in the car drove toward the park with Charlie and Marie following behind.

The ride to the park was quiet—unnervingly quiet. Billy sat in the passenger seat looking blankly out of the window, and Darryl found himself looking over at his lover constantly. But he didn't know what to say to him as he tried to understand the anguish Billy was going through.

Pulling into the park, Darryl parked and got out, but Billy sat where he was and didn't move. The Hanovers' car pulled up next to them, and the boys practically sprang out of the backseat, running to the water's edge with their bags of bread swinging beside them. "Come on, Billy," Darryl prodded lightly, but he just shook his head, and Darryl saw a tear run down his cheek. Darryl leaned across the seat and wiped it away with his thumb.

"I'm really going to lose them, aren't I?" Billy took a heaving breath. "Up to now, I guess I held out hope for some miracle, but it's not going to happen, is it?" Billy turned toward him, clearly anguished. "Look at them." Darryl let his gaze slide away from Billy to where Davey and Donnie were throwing bits of bread to the birds, the boys laughing as the birds fought, squawked, and quacked over the food. "They're having such fun. Do you remember how just a little while ago, they were having the same fun with us?" Billy covered his eyes, and the tears began to flow in earnest.

Darryl wanted to cry himself. He thought he was going to miss those boys almost as much as Billy, but he knew he had to stay strong. "And they will again. You know those boys may be small, but their hearts are big enough to love you, me, and them all at the same time. Our job right now is to make sure they feel comfortable enough with the Hanovers to be able to start a life with them."

A soft rap on the window caught their attention. Marie stood outside Billy's door, and he lowered the window. "Please join us. The boys are asking for both of you." Darryl opened his door and climbed out of the car, but Billy stayed where he was. Darryl didn't want to leave Billy alone in the car. Marie walked around to where Darryl was standing. "Let me talk to him," she said softly, and Darryl nodded, leaving the door open and walking to where Charlie and the boys were playing.

"Is Biwwy okay?" Davey asked as he looked toward the car.

"He's just a little sad, but he'll be okay."

"Davey," Donnie called, "look at the white one!" Donnie pointed toward a duck with stark white feathers, and both boys began throwing bread in its direction, yelling when he actually ate some of the bread.

Darryl saw Charlie standing off to the side, watching the boys, and Darryl went to stand next to him. "What is it you do, Charlie?"

"I'm a naval commander. When I was younger, I traveled the world on the biggest ships you can imagine, but now I help manage naval supplies." Charlie looked toward the car, and Darryl followed his gaze. The doors were closed, and Marie seemed to be talking to Billy. "What do you do?"

Darryl pulled his eyes away, watching the boys again. "I own a restaurant in town. I met Billy when he asked for a job." Darryl couldn't help looking back toward the car. This time he saw what looked like Billy talking and both of them wiping their eyes. "Do you move around a lot?"

"I used to," Charlie answered, taking the piece of bread Donnie gave him and throwing it into the water. "But not so much anymore. Marie and I have a quiet life now." He smiled. "Or *had*." The smile told Darryl that he wasn't lamenting what was going to be a drastic change in the least. "We have a house with plenty of room and a big backyard. We bought it when Marie was pregnant, and getting someplace smaller seemed like giving up hope."

"Can I ask you something personal?" Charlie nodded in response to Darryl's question. "How come you aren't angrier about what happened?"

"You mean why aren't we angry with Billy?" Charlie clarified, and it was Darryl's turn to nod. "Oh, I was. For a long time, I was angry, bitter—you name it. Every time I saw Marie cry for her children, I wanted to punch the walls. For years I blamed the hospital, and then I blamed myself for not watching over my children. After the babies were taken somehow, it took time to figure things out, and by then they were gone without a trace." The strong man blinked hard, obviously trying to cover his tears. "But I don't blame Billy. He didn't do anything except raise my sons and keep them safe."

Charlie sighed, his eyes filled with relieved sadness. "For five years we wondered what happened to them. Were they okay? Were they being loved? There wasn't a day in five years that Marie didn't mention her babies." Charlie huffed softly, watching the boys drown bread. "The nursery was set up just as it was for almost three years." Darryl saw him swallow hard, both men dealing with the lumps in their throats. "When we got the call that our babies had been found, it seemed almost too good to be true. I wouldn't let myself believe it could be true until we actually saw the boys."

"Can we go play in the fort?" Donnie asked, looking up at him.

Darryl looked over to Charlie, who answered, "Of course, but look before crossing the drive."

Davey took Donnie's hand, and together the two men watched as the boys crossed the empty drive before running across the grass toward the fort. "We should keep an eye on them," Darryl commented as he again looked toward the car.

"They'll be fine." Charlie started walked in the direction of the play fort. "I can imagine what Billy must be feeling, but if anyone can help him, it's Marie. She understands what he's going through."

Darryl looked again. The two of them were talking earnestly, both wiping their eyes. "I think you're right." They stood quietly for a few seconds. "Ever since we found out about the boys...." Darryl swallowed, hoping what he wanted to say came out right. "Billy has probably slept through the night once. Most of the time, he sits up and worries."

"We went through that for months. But you know, I never thought that as happy as we are to have our sons back, that someone else would be equally upset to let them go. It sort of tempers the joy." Darryl gaped in near wonder at the way he hit the nail on the head. These were special people.

The boys began calling to them as they raced inside the fort. Darryl and Charlie walked to where they were playing, sitting at one of the nearby picnic tables.

"Can I ask you something?"

Darryl smiled. "Turnabout is fair play."

"Are you and Billy a couple?" Charlie seemed slightly embarrassed by the question.

Darryl studied him for a second, but he didn't see anything other than curiosity. "Yes. We haven't been together long, but yes, we are. Is that a problem?"

"No. Not at all." The boys calling drew their attention for a while. "I'm glad they had both of you."

Darryl thought that now might be an opportunity to feel them out. "Now they'll have the four of us." He knew that Billy's biggest fear now was that he wouldn't be allowed to see his brothers again.

"Yes, I suppose they will," Charlie said as he watched the boys playing.

Darryl looked back toward the car and saw Billy and Marie walking toward them. Billy actually looked less miserable, the two of them continuing to talk as they approached the picnic table.

"Biwwy!" Davey rushed out of the fort, running across the grass and grabbing Billy's arm. "Will you push me on the swings?"

"Me too!" Donnie called as he followed behind.

Billy looked to Marie, who smiled. "Go on. They want their brother to push them." Billy smiled at her and led the boys to the swings, and Darryl swallowed around the lump in his throat and felt the knot that had been in his stomach since yesterday start to unwind. There were plenty of hard days ahead, but things would work out.

CHAPTER THIRTEEN

BILLY stared at the ceiling, listening to Darryl's soft breathing next to him, one of his lover's arms wound around his waist. For the past week, Darryl had slept every night with his arm around him, holding him. Billy knew it was his way of trying to make him feel safe and making sure he didn't feel so alone. Billy rolled onto his side and watched as Darryl slept.

"Try to sleep, babe." Darryl's eyes didn't open, and Billy felt himself tugged closer, Darryl sliding a leg between his, their hips coming together.

Sleep was the one thing he couldn't do. Today was the day Donnie and Davey left town with their parents. God, he hated to think of Marie and Charlie like that, but he had to face facts—Davey and Donnie were their children, and as much as it hurt, he had to let them go. Besides Darryl, who'd been a rock throughout this whole thing, the only other thing that was making this remotely bearable was the fact that he actually liked the Hanovers. They were nice people who'd gone out of their way to let Billy know that the boys were still his brothers and that they wanted him to be a part of the twins' lives.

"What is it?" Darryl's eyes slid open, and Billy felt like he always felt when Darryl looked at him like that.

"Nothing new." Billy felt himself being tugged closer. "Just that by the end of the day, the boys will be three hundred miles away."

"They asked me today if they could take their racecar beds with them, along with Gordon and Anna." Billy felt Darryl's breath against his skin.

"What'd you tell them?"

"Nothing. Charlie said that their racecar beds needed to stay here so they'd have somewhere to sleep when they came to visit."

Billy propped himself up on his elbow. "Did he really say that?" He wanted to believe it so badly. Throughout the last week, Marie and Charlie had made a continual point of referring to Billy as the twins' brother, but truthfully, he figured it was mostly lip service for the twins' benefit.

"Of course he did. Charlie also told me that they want you to come for visits as well." Billy felt Darryl start to suck at that spot on his shoulder. "We'll go see the twins, and they'll come up here. Think of today as 'until we meet again' as opposed to 'goodbye', because I'm sure you'll be seeing them often."

"I know." Billy sniffled involuntarily. "Sometimes I think they'll be better off with them than they have been with me." Tears welled in his eyes, and he tried in vain to stop them. "At least with the Hanovers, they won't have to worry about getting enough to eat or having a safe place to live, like they did with me." He began to shake.

"Shhh," Darryl soothed gently. "You gave then a home full of love, whether it was here or at the Molly." Billy felt Darryl's weight shift them both on the bed until he was on his back, with Darryl looking down into his eyes. "You filled my home with love as well, and I don't want anyone disparaging the man I love... and that includes you." Billy felt Darryl's body react to their proximity, and he knew Darryl meant what he said. But his own body did nothing, and he looked away. "It's okay. You've got a lot on your mind right now." Darryl captured his lips, and Billy closed his eyes, letting the love he was being shown and the love he felt deep in his heart relax away some of the anxiety.

"I do love you, Darryl." He'd felt so out of control for most of the past week. The boys had been gradually spending more and more time with Marie and Charlie. For the last two nights, they'd been staying with them at their hotel. He'd seen them every day when they came into the restaurant for lunch and during the afternoons between lunch and dinner. Two days ago, he'd heard Davey call Marie "Mommy" for the first time, and he'd had to excuse himself and rush to the bathroom as the tears began to well. In his mind, he'd always seen his mother in the boys, and hearing them call someone else "Mommy" had brought up a rush of old pain that he'd barely been able to control.

"They'll be over here for breakfast in a few hours." Darryl's voice pulled him out of his thoughts, and a thumb wiped away the tear his thoughts conjured up. "What are you thinking about?"

"My mom."

Darryl slipped off his body and back onto the mattress before tugging him close. "There's a lot of pain inside you, isn't there?" A hand stroked along his arm.

"No more than you went through with Connor. The pain's the same, even if the circumstances are different," Billy whispered softly.

"Except that your pain is happening now, and mine is in the past." Darryl kept rubbing his arm. "You aren't alone."

"I know. That's one thing I never doubted."

"Good." Darryl's lips traveled over his shoulder, and Billy felt his eyes close on their own.

The next thing Billy knew, Darryl was getting out of bed, and then the covers were pulled up over him and he fell back to sleep. Soon, the scent of fresh coffee and bacon roused him out of bed and into the bathroom. He'd just finished dressing when he heard the front door bang open and little feet running through the house. A few minutes later, he'd been found and was hugged to within an inch of his life.

"Mom and Dad say that we're going to our new house today," Davey said as he and Donnie tugged him down the stairs. "Are you coming too?"

The question took Billy completely by surprise, and he swallowed hard. "No." Billy stopped and knelt down to their level. "You two"—he hugged them tight—"are going to live with your mom and dad. I'm staying here with Uncle Darryl." He really thought they'd understood all this. "You wouldn't want him to be lonely."

The boys began to cry, holding on to him tightly. "I want you to go wif us," Davey whined through his tears, while Donnie just buried his head against his older brother's shoulder, crying softly. Billy's emotions had been near the surface all week, but to his surprise, he didn't feel tears pushing up like he would have expected. He had to be there for the boys, and that gave him strength.

"That's enough of that," Billy coaxed softly, and Donnie lifted his head, rubbing his wet little face. "You're going to be with your mom and dad. In a few months you'll be in school like the big boys you are. There'll be other kids to play with, and I'll come to visit, and you'll come here too." Their eyes got wide as if they didn't believe him. "You have to come back to check on Gordon and Anna. They'll miss you." Billy knew that wasn't exactly true and actually felt a smile break out on his face as he thought of the boys trying to pet Darryl's koi. "Your mom and dad love you, just like I do, and nothing's going to change that." The boys' tears began to dry up, and Billy stood, each twin taking a hand.

"Will my racecar bed still be here?" Donnie asked quietly.

"Where else are you gonna sleep when you come stay?" Billy asked as he ruffled his brother's hair before changing the subject.

"I'm hungry—are you both ready to eat?" Hand in hand, they went down the stairs and into the dining room.

Charlie and Marie were already at the table. The boys took their places on either side of Billy as Darryl began bringing in the food. "Charlie and I were just saying this morning that it's a shame that we don't live closer together." She placed her napkin on her lap, and to Billy's surprise, he saw the boys do the same. "I hope you'll be able to come for a visit soon." From her expression, Billy had no doubt she was sincere. Her eyes were so earnest, and over the past week, Billy had come to realize that Marie was one of the sweetest people. She'd actually asked if she could use their kitchen a few days earlier and had baked cookies for the boys, leaving a plate on the counter for him and Darryl. The boys were already taken with both her and Charlie.

Billy sighed to himself, because he'd wished the same thing, but it was Darryl who actually answered her. "We'll be down to visit the boys often enough." Billy saw him smile at him before turning to Marie. "You'll probably get sick of us."

Marie made an unladylike noise, snorting softly in disbelief, and the boys began to laugh, pointing at her with huge grins on their faces. Marie joined them, covering her mouth and turning red. The rest followed suit, and Billy felt some of the tension he'd been carrying slip away.

The rest of breakfast passed quickly—too quickly. Billy and Darryl helped Charlie load the last of the boys' things in the car, and everyone stood at the curb, unsure of what to do. Davey and Donnie gave him big hugs again and again before doing the same with Darryl and climbing in the backseat of the car.

Billy found himself staring at Marie and Charlie, unsure of what to say. It was Marie who made the first move, stepping forward and hugging Billy to her. "Thank you," she whispered into his ear before releasing him and giving Darryl a hug as well.

Charlie shook hands with both of them. "I can't thank you two enough... for everything," Charlie said, a little choked up. "You have our numbers and address." He walked around to the driver's side door. "We'll see you both very soon." He raised his hand and then climbed into the car. The door thunked closed, and Billy saw the boys waving from the backseat. Billy and Darryl waved back as the engine started and the car pulled away from the curb. Billy kept waving until the car turned the corner. Letting his arm fall still, he stood staring toward the corner until Darryl's arms pulled him into a hug.

"You going to be okay?" Darryl asked softly as they headed toward the front door.

Billy nodded against Darryl's chest. "I think so." He didn't feel weepy, just sort of empty and drained. "It's been a long week." Timewise, the week had flown by, but emotionally, it felt as though he'd been through the wringer. They stepped into the house, and Darryl closed the door behind them. "We should get in to work. I'll get things cleaned up in the kitchen while you get changed."

"Are you sure? You could stay home today if you need to." Darryl's voice was full of concern.

"No." Billy stood in the hallway. "I need to keep busy." Darryl kissed him softly and went upstairs while Billy walked into the dining room, carrying the dishes to the kitchen, loading them in the dishwasher. Billy heard Darryl's feet on the stairs as he was finishing up.

Billy didn't feel like talking on the walk to the restaurant, and thankfully Darryl didn't press him. Sebastian was already at work, and after getting a quick kiss from Darryl, Billy joined Sebastian, making sure everything was set up for lunch. Just before opening, the other servers and the bussers arrived.

The doors opened on time, and Billy was glad they were very busy. He didn't have time to think between taking orders, running for drinks and extra napkins, cleaning up drink spills, and retrieving completed orders. Everything seemed to happen this particular shift, and before he knew it, the dining room had emptied out again.

"Are you okay?" Sebastian startled him a little as he was setting up tables for dinner. "You ran like crazy the entire shift. You can ask for help if you need it," Sebastian reminded him gently.

"I know. I think I just need to be busy right now. The boys left this morning."

Sebastian nodded slowly, placing a hand on his shoulder. "If you want to talk, I'll listen anytime, you know that." He looked around to make sure they were alone. "I know you have Darryl, but sometimes it's easier to talk to someone else."

"Thanks, Sebastian, I appreciate it." Billy didn't really want to talk to anyone right now. He'd talked about the boys leaving so much that he just wanted to talk about something else for a little while. "How are things with you?"

"Same, same, you know. Nothing really changes much around here," Sebastian said as he drifted away, and Billy went right back to work, keeping himself busy. Once there were no more salt shakers to fill or napkins to fold, he began looking around.

"When you get around to organizing the beer bottles in the cooler by size and bottle color, I'll know you've gone 'round the bend," Sebastian teased from across the room.

Realizing Sebastian was right, that he was going overboard, Billy wandered into the kitchen, only to see Darryl apparently wiping down his already clean work area. "You doing the same thing I am—trying to keep busy?"

"Yeah." Darryl dropped his cloth in the sanitizing water and then wrung it out, carrying the container back to the dish room and dumping it down the drain. Setting the pan down to be washed, Darryl added, "Three times, I found myself going back to the office only to realize I was going to check on the boys."

"I know," Billy said, the thoughts he'd been suppressing catching up with him. "I found myself doing the same thing. Keeping busy seems to be the one things that works, at least for now."

"Yeah, it does." Darryl gave him a hug, and Billy let himself relax against his lover's warmth.

"I'm sorry. I've been neglecting you." Billy tilted his head up for a kiss. Over the last week, they'd cuddled a lot, and their kisses had been sweet and tender but soft—meant to comfort rather than inspire passion. This time, Billy felt Darryl's hands slide along his cheeks and his lips were taken hard, restarting a fire inside him that felt as though it'd gone out for a while.

"You haven't been neglecting me; you've been hurting. But tonight, now that the house is quiet, I intend to show you just much you mean to me and see just how loud I can make you scream." Darryl leered at him, eyes smoldering, and Billy felt his insides begin to swirl. Their eyes locked, and Billy felt everything slip away—the worry, the sadness, everything. For a few seconds, he was lost in Darryl's deep brown eyes. "You've spent years caring for everyone else in your life, and now it's time someone took care of you."

Billy's body throbbed, and he squirmed as his pants became way too tight. He was so hard he ached, his balls drawing tight against his body. "Darryl," he moaned softly before his lips were taken again.

Slowly, awareness of the things around him returned as Darryl's kiss subsided and his lips slipped away. Billy's knees felt a little weak, and he was grateful for the wall that Darryl had him pressed against—otherwise he'd be a heap on the floor. Chest heaving, he looked around to see if anyone had noticed. Everyone in the kitchen was obviously trying to ignore them, so yeah, they'd noticed.

Darryl seemed completely unconcerned. "That was just a taste," he said as he backed away. "You'll get the rest tonight."

Billy nodded, unable to talk, and watched as Darryl leered, eyes raking over him before returning to his station. Billy heaved for breath for a few minutes before pulling his eyes away from his magnetic lover. Stepping inside the nearest room to hide the obscene bulge in his pants, Billy found himself in the one place he'd been trying to avoid all day: the office.

In his mind, it was still the boys' domain, and he had to force himself to call it the office. Over the past week, the boys had spent less and less time in the room, but their presence was still everywhere, from the toys overflowing the box in the corner, to the crayon pictures that decorated the walls, to the television and DVD player with dozens of kid-friendly shows stacked below on the stand. Everyone in the restaurant had brought in things for them. His first thought was to take everything down, box up the toys, and return the room to the way it had been before the boys had taken over, but he just couldn't bring himself to do it. If their things were here, then they were still here in some way.

"Why don't you pack up the toys and put them in the trunk? We can put them away at the house," Darryl said softly from behind him.

"What about the rest?" Billy felt himself getting choked up again.

"Leave it. I like the pictures, and they remind me of them." He heard Darryl's voice catch and almost went to him, but he knew if he did, he'd start crying again, and there was no use in that. It wasn't going to bring them back, and it wasn't going to help. "And I'm hoping they'll send more." Darryl turned away, and Billy thought for a few minutes before deciding Darryl was right. Going out back, he found a few boxes and returned to the room to get to work.

With the toys packed in the boxes and loaded into the car, Billy returned to check the room one more time. As he bent down to look under the futon, a paper dropped from his pocket. Picking it up, he saw that it was the Hanovers' address in Richmond. Getting up, dying of curiosity, he sat at the desk and moved the mouse to turn on the screen. He wasn't really sure how to get what he wanted, but then he saw an icon labeled "Google Earth."

Billy clicked on it, and the computer opened a window showing the entire United States. There was a box in the corner, and

Billy typed the Hanovers' address one letter at a time. He'd only used a computer a few times, but it seemed easy. When he pressed "enter," the computer screen zoomed in, getting closer and closer. States appeared, and then rivers and mountains. Getting closer still, Billy saw streets and finally houses, and then it stopped over what looked like a ranch-style house with what indeed looked like a big backyard. He was amazed at the details he could make out and half expected to see people coming and going. Behind the house, not too far away, he noticed what looked like a playground and maybe a school. It seemed idyllic.

As he moved around, a box popped up. "Moving to the area? Click here for houses and apartments." Curious, he clicked on it. A page came up, and Billy clicked on "apartments." A whole list appeared on the screen with pictures and everything. These sure looked a hell of a lot nicer than the ones he'd lived in. A button displayed beside each picture read "Request Further Information."

He'd have been lying to himself if he didn't at least admit that he'd thought about moving to follow the twins, and this was tempting. At one point, he'd even asked Marie about apartments in the area where they lived. She'd told him what he'd wanted to know and then added, "Billy, you can't live the rest of your life for your brothers. They love you and you love them, but honey, you need to move on with your own life. You have someone here who loves you very much. Don't throw that away." She'd been so sincere and caring that it had made him stop and think.

He saw an ad for a small apartment that caught his eye. Clicking on the button, he got more pictures and plenty of information. He read it over for a few minutes and then closed the window, clicking on a few more. For a while, he let himself wonder what it would be like. The apartments seemed nice, and he let himself imagine being near the twins. "Jesus," he muttered to himself before shaking his head and closing the window, making sure the computer looked the way he'd found it. Marie was right—it was time he moved on with his life. The boys would always be a part of his life, but they couldn't be his whole life. Darryl loved him.

Feeling decidedly guilty, he pushed the chair back from the desk and walked back out through the kitchen. He saw Darryl working, and another pang of guilt raced through him. How could he think of leaving Darryl? The man loved him, had given him a job and a home. How could he do that to Darryl? Hell, the man could make him forget his own name, he loved him so intensely, and Billy loved him just as much. Billy let himself think of how he'd feel if he no longer had Darryl, and the thought left him feeling ice-cold.

Positive that Darryl could read his emotions on his face, he hurried out of the kitchen and into the dining room to get back to work.

CHAPTER FOURTEEN

DARRYL watched Billy walk through the kitchen. The man couldn't even look at him, didn't even have the courage to face him. Granted, he'd been afraid that this was what Billy would do. "What's got your knickers in a twist?" Maureen teased quietly from behind him.

"Billy was in the office looking at apartments in Richmond," he said, almost under his breath.

She stopped cleaning her work boards, all teasing gone from her expression. "What did he say about it?"

Darryl's hands stopped in mid-chop. "Nothing. I didn't ask him. I went in the office to see how he was doing and saw him looking at apartments on the Internet. I just left." He set the knife aside and turned toward her. "I guess I should have known this was coming." Butterflies started in his stomach.

"What?" He felt a cloth hit him on the shoulder. "Why on earth would you say that?"

"He's twenty-one and I'm thirty. To him, I must seem like an old man. Besides, he was asking Marie about apartments earlier in the week." Darryl turned to face her, feeling the butterflies turn to weights. "With the twins leaving, I guess I should have figured there was a chance he'd follow them. They're all the family he has."

"He hasn't told you he's leaving, has he?"

"No, but he looked really guilty as he walked through the kitchen."

"Just ask him." Maureen went back to her cleaning. "It's probably nothing."

"I hope so." Darryl picked up his knife again and went back to chopping vegetables.

"Am I ever wrong?" Maureen quipped, and Darryl turned around to leer at her and remind her of the numerous times she'd asked his advice when she and Eric had started dating. "Let me have a few delusions, will ya?" She smiled, and Darryl let his attention return to his work. She was probably right. Billy was probably just curious about the area where the twins were going to live.

Dinner was hectic as hell, and Darryl thought that he'd never been so happy to see a day end. He'd tried to talk to Billy, but the younger man had always seemed too busy, either working with Sebastian or seeing to his tables. A few times, Darryl had almost pulled him into the office to ask him what was going on, but frankly, he'd chickened out. Locking the back door, he and Billy left the now-dark restaurant and headed for home.

Nearly deserted, silent sidewalks passed beneath their feet during the walk home. A few times, Darryl tried to ask Billy what was going on but stopped, his hands stuffed in his pockets.

Darryl unlocked the house and walked straight upstairs to their room. He was so tired, physically and emotionally, that he could barely move. Getting undressed, he crawled between the covers and almost didn't feel Billy get into bed with him. "Did I do something wrong?" Billy asked quietly from behind him. "You haven't said a thing to me all evening unless it's to bark something at me about an order or something I forgot." Billy definitely sounded hurt, but Darryl didn't roll over or say anything, he just closed his eyes, feeling self-righteously hurt himself.

Darryl closed his eyes and sighed softly to himself, trying to fall asleep. The bed vibrating softly caught his attention, and he stilled even his breathing. A soft gasp from next to him made him start to worry, and he rolled over. In the dim room, he could see Billy's head buried in the pillow, his shoulders raising and lowering. He was crying. All Darryl's hurt drained away, and he curled closer to Billy, cradling him in his arms. "Don't cry, love."

"What'd I do?" Billy half squeaked as he looked at him.

"Are you moving to Richmond?" Darryl blurted out. "I saw you looking at apartments this afternoon."

Billy wiped his eyes. "Is that what this is about? I was looking at this program that showed me where the twins will be living and saw an advertisement, so I looked at it. I was seeing if things were nice where they'd be living." He sniffled and glared down at him. "Is that what this is all about? Why didn't you just ask?" Billy slapped him on the shoulder. "You big lug!"

"You looked so guilty and wouldn't look at me." Darryl actually whined slightly.

"Because I felt guilty. I did look at apartments, and I felt bad for doing it." Darryl felt Billy's hand slide along his arm. "I love you. I thought about moving to be closer to the twins, but then I'd have to leave you, and I couldn't do that."

Darryl tugged Billy closer, his stomach easing for the first time in hours. "You aren't leaving?"

"No. I have no intention of going anywhere, unless you want me to." Billy nestled closer, and Darryl's lips brushed over his shoulder, the taste of Billy's skin bursting on his tongue. "I guess we need to learn to talk about these kinds of things."

"I guess so." Darryl kissed him some more.

"Why would you think I wouldn't talk to you before making a decision like that?"

Darryl stopped what he was doing, looking into Billy's eyes shining with light reflected from outside. "Why do you think? Your twenty-one, I'm thirty. I keep wondering when you're going to wake up and realize you don't need the old guy and want someone younger."

"Why would you think that?" Billy arched his neck, and Darryl took advantage of the invitation.

"Have you looked at yourself in the mirror?" Darryl started sucking and kissing at the base of his lover's neck. "You're beautiful"—Darryl kept kissing—"with beautiful eyes and kissable lips." Darryl captured those lips, shifting on the bed so that Billy was beneath him. "I believe I promised you something earlier."

"Uh-huh," Billy responded as Darryl took his lips again, pressing his younger lover between the mattress and his skin. Darryl could feel Billy's excitement throughout his entire body. Billy practically vibrated with it as Darryl's hands slid over warm, smooth skin. The past week had been tough on both of them, neither in the mood for much more than a cuddle, but being this close to Billy, hearing those small noises, feeling that skin against his, had Darryl's mind reeling. His thoughts were clouded by need, desire, and downright lust. He needed this man like he needed air to breathe. "Darryl," Billy gasped as he heaved for breath. "Need you."

"I know, love, I need you too."

Billy stilled, and Darryl stopped his kissing, looking his lover in the eye. "No, I mean I need you always."

Darryl's heart soared, and he tightened his grip on his lover, pulling Billy to him, their bodies meeting from chest to toe. Billy needed him, and Billy had chosen him. That was all he needed to know. Rolling them on the bed, Darryl relished Billy's weight on top of him. Holding his lover's butt, Darryl felt Billy kiss him, lips roaming over his neck and chest. When Billy latched onto one of his nipples, Darryl growled low. When Billy bit lightly, Darryl cried out, and when Billy slid down his body, taking him deep, Darryl thought his head would explode. "Billy, so good."

His fingers slid through soft hair as Billy's head bobbed and the smaller man made humming sounds, sucking Darryl's shaft and teasing him with his tongue. "Please, Billy." Darryl gently withdrew, and Billy whined softly. "I want to be inside you."

Billy nodded, and Darryl reached to the stand for the supplies. Billy took the lube, and Darryl heard the sexiest sounds. Billy moaned softly, and Darryl knew what was happening; he only wished he could see Billy's fingers buried in that young, lithe body. After Darryl rolled on a condom, Billy straddled him, and Darryl slowly entered his lover.

The heat engulfed him and the grip squeezed him as Darryl was surrounded by Billy. "Love you," Darryl groaned as he was taken deeper, fingers gripping Billy's thighs for dear life. Then he felt Billy's butt against his hips, and Darryl knew he'd reached heaven. "You okay?" Darryl's mind cleared just enough to see the blissful look on Billy's face as he began to move, slowly raising and lowering his body. Hands slid along Darryl's chest. Leaning forward, Darryl captured Billy's lips and held him tight, their spirits linked along with their bodies. "You chose me," Darryl sighed against Billy's lips. "You really chose me."

"I did, and you chose me." Billy smiled and wiggled his butt as he pushed Darryl back onto the mattress, quickening his pace. Darryl picked up Billy's rhythm, their bodies meeting.

"Fuck, that's hot!" Darryl groaned loudly as he watched Billy's hand glide along his shaft, that tight body undulating as he rode Darryl. The room filled with their sounds of love, their passion building with each of Billy's slow, long movements.

Billy's pace was driving him crazy. Unable to take it anymore, Darryl withdrew and captured Billy around the waist, tumbling him onto the bed.

"Darryl," he cried out in frustration.

"I've got you." Kneeing Billy's legs apart, he lifted them, resting Billy's feet on his shoulders, and he re-entered his lover in a single powerful thrust.

Billy cried out, and for a second Darryl thought he might have hurt him. He stilled, only to get a snarled groan of frustration in return. "Do it!"

Darryl did, driving deep, Billy crying out each time their bodies came together. Darryl could see Billy's head rocking, feel him meet every movement, hear him filling the room with his passion, the cries fueling their mutual desire. For Darryl, this wasn't sex, this was staking his claim—permanently, he hoped. "Mine!" Darryl vocalized his thoughts as he pounded into Billy. Realizing what he was doing, he let up, only to have Billy grab the back of his legs, pressing him forward. His little man wanted more, everything he could give. "You're mine, Billy!"

"And… you're… mine!" Billy gasped as Darryl thrust deep and hard, their bodies shaking the bed, banging it against the wall. "Tell me, Darryl!"

"I'm yours," he cried as his body reacted to Billy's emotions. Darryl felt everything clench, and he thrust deep, stopping as he poured himself into his lover. His head spun, and he gasped for breath as he felt Billy clench around him, the cries of his sweet lover filling the room and his heart.

Darryl barely had the energy to move. Both he and Billy were covered in sweat. Gasping softly, he slid from Billy's body. Sliding off the bed, Darryl walked to the bathroom, disposing of things and starting the shower. In the bedroom, Billy hadn't moved, and Darryl coaxed him off the bed and under the streaming water. Billy appeared drained and half asleep as he held on, and Darryl slowly, tenderly washed his lover's body.

Turning off the water, he helped Billy back to bed. "Night, love." In answer, Billy curled closer to him, making a soft sound in his throat. In a few minutes, Billy's breathing evened out and he was asleep, snoring lightly, head resting against Darryl's shoulder. Closing his eyes, Darryl held Billy as he, too, drifted to sleep.

DARRYL woke, expecting to get pounced on at any moment, and remembered that the boys weren't in the house any more. The quiet was going to take some getting used to. Before Billy, Davey, and Donnie had moved in, the house had always been like this, and frankly, he missed the activity. The one thing he wasn't missing was Billy. He was right next to him, looking up at him, eyes blazing with a heat that made Darryl shudder. "You want something?" Darryl smirked before Billy kissed it away.

"Yeah. Can I make love to you?" Billy's hand slid down Darryl's chest, teasing him a little before going lower. "What's wrong?"

Darryl wanted to die of embarrassment. "I haven't done that since...." Fuck, he thought he'd left all this behind.

"Connor?" Billy supplied, and Darryl nodded. He hadn't realized how much that was still with him. He hadn't thought about all that in weeks, and he'd actually believed Billy's love had banished all that old crap. He should have known it wouldn't be that easy. "It's okay." Billy leaned close, his lips brushing over Darryl's as the bigger man felt Billy tug him on top, legs wrapping around his waist. "You are what matters," Billy told him with a wriggle of his hips.

Darryl wasn't so sure, but Billy's lips did a great job pushing those worries to the back of his mind, that sweet body rubbing against his, long fingers easily coaxing his body to life. Jesus, how could he possibly think of anything or anyone else when Billy did that? The answer was that he couldn't—not when there was all that tasty skin beneath him, waiting for him, Billy wanting him. Billy began stroking slowly, and Darryl hissed through his teeth, his abdomen clenching, just before the fingers slipped away again. "You're teasing me?"

Then the phone began to ring, and Darryl huffed against Billy's lips. He was tempted to try ignoring it, but it just wasn't working, and he gave up with a sigh, rolling onto the mattress and answering the phone.

"Uncle Dawwyl?" He knew it was one of the boys and couldn't suppress a smile.

"Yes, it's me." He motioned to Billy, who raced out of the room and picked up the other extension a few seconds later. "How was the trip? Did you have a fun ride?"

"Uh-huh." He heard a slight sputtering on the other end of the line, and he knew it had to be Davey; he did that whenever he got excited. "They got Donnie and me racecar beds! Dad said they ordered them just for us!" He could practically see the youngster jumping for joy. "And we each got our own room, but Donnie slept in mine anyway." He barely took time to breathe. "There's swings in the backyard and everything."

"Hi, Davey," Billy said as Davey finally took a breath.

"Biwwy!" he screamed into the phone. "When are you coming to see us? They got everything here."

"In a few weeks. Both Uncle Darryl and I are going to come visit you." Billy's excitement was tinged with a touch of sadness. "And you can show us everything."

"'Kay." He was quiet for a while. "Love you." The phone line filled with noises for a few minutes.

"Biwwy," Donnie's more timid voice came through the line, "I had bad dreams."

"Did you hold Davey's hand?"

"Uh-huh." His voice was garbled.

"Are you sucking your thumb?" Billy asked, but there was no response. "I can't hear your head nod," Billy prompted gently.

"Uh-huh."

"You know that big boys don't suck their thumbs," Billy explained gently. "Do you want to tell me about it?"

Silence. "I don't remember it."

"Did Mom sit with you?" Darryl wished Billy was in the room with him.

"No, Dad did." Darryl could almost see Donnie standing by the phone in his pajamas, holding the receiver with both hands.

"Did he make it better?"

"Yes."

"So you'll be okay?"

"Yeah, but I miss you. He doesn't make the monsters go away as good as you."

"Your dad's big and strong. The monsters are afraid of him."

"Oh." Donnie's voice lilted upwards. "That's okay, then." A voice in the background said something, obviously Marie. "Bye, Biwwy." Donnie sounded happier.

"Hello." Marie's voice came through the line. "We made it home late yesterday, or we'd have called last night. Both boys seem to be settling in." She stopped for a few seconds, obviously unsure of what to say.

It was Billy who answered. "They seem just fine."

"Are you still coming to visit in a few weeks?"

Darryl spoke up. "Yes. We'll call you in a few days with our exact plans. We need to find a hotel in your area."

"That's not necessary. We have room, and the boys will want to spend all the time they can with you." She sounded a little nervous to Darryl, which was probably natural under the circumstances.

"Thank you. We'll talk in a few days." Darryl said goodbye and hung up. He could still hear Billy's voice drifting up from downstairs, and he figured he and Marie were talking, which was very good. Getting out of bed, he walked to the bathroom to clean up.

Billy joined him a few minutes later, smiling. "I think they're going to be okay," Billy pronounced as he started the shower.

"How about you—are you going to be okay?" Darryl finished shaving and stepped under the water, with Billy following behind him.

"God, I hope so." Billy clung to him as the water surged over their bodies, erections rubbing across soft skin.

"Unfortunately, as much as I'd love a round of shower sex, we have to be at the restaurant in twenty minutes. But I promise I'll make it up to you." Darryl let his hands wander over Billy's back and down to his butt.

"It was *my* brothers who called and interrupted," Billy answered softly, his lips so close Darryl could feel the heat of his breath. "Maybe"—Billy hands slid to Darryl's butt, making him tense a little—"I should be making it up to you."

"I can accept that," Darryl answered with a smile before capturing Billy's lips. "Oh, fuck, I think we're going to be late this morning after all." Darryl kissed Billy again, pressing him against the shower wall, hands roaming over all that smooth, wet skin.

CHAPTER FIFTEEN

BILLY pulled open the back door of the restaurant and rushed inside, looking around for Darryl, finding him sitting at a table working on paperwork, drinking a cup of coffee. "Where'd you go?"

"I stopped home to check the mail." Billy grinned as he set a large manila envelope on the table.

Darryl set his things aside, looking back at Billy with a huge smile. "Is that what I think it is?"

"See for yourself." Billy unclasped the loosely closed envelope and drew out world-class works of art, at least in their eyes. "I thought these could go on the refrigerator."

"But what about the ones already there?" Darryl teased. The walls in the office were covered with drawings, as was the refrigerator and every other place they could think of. Once they were put up, neither of them wanted to take them down. "Maybe we can put some of them in an album."

Billy got up and walked to the office, returning a few minutes later with a large scrapbook album. "Like this one?" Billy handed it to Darryl. "I thought we could put the drawings in it together." Billy could hardly contain his energy. Ever since their visit to see the boys a few weeks earlier, when both Donnie and Davey had handed each of them a stack of their drawings, telling them about each and every one, an envelope had arrived about once a week with more drawings. Billy figured that in a few months, school papers would join the drawings.

"You have to hand it to Marie, she and Charlie have been wonderful."

"Speaking of them…." Billy slipped into the booth, nudging Darryl over. "There was a message from her asking if it would be okay if they brought the boys up for a visit in a few weeks. I called her back and told her of course. She told the boys, and we got cheers."

Billy felt Darryl's hand slide over his leg, squeezing gently. "So tell me why you really went home?" Fuck, the man could see through everything he did.

"Okay, fine. I had something I needed to do, Mr. Nosy." God, Billy hoped Darryl wouldn't push too hard. He hated keeping secrets from Darryl, but this was the only way he could think of.

"Fine, don't tell me." Darryl nudged him so he could get out. "I need to get back to work." Billy didn't move, and Darryl stared at him. "Are you going to let me out?"

"If you pay the toll." Billy leaned closer, and Darryl finally got the hint and kissed him. Billy returned it, nestling close to Darryl's chest, glad he'd been able to distract the man. "You've been so good to me."

"Where is this coming from?" Darryl said as he half smiled suspiciously.

A knock on the front door interrupted them, and Darryl looked up. "Could you please tell them we're closed until dinner?"

"I love you, Darryl, and I think he may be here to see you."

Daryl took another look at the man standing at the front door.

Billy got up and unlocked the front door, noticing the man's gaze never left Darryl. "I see you found it okay," Billy said, and the man nodded, taking a few steps inside.

"Yes, thank you," he said softly to Billy, looking like he would bolt at any time. "Darryl, I know I've changed...."

Billy saw his lover's eyes widen in sudden recognition. "Connor?" Darryl asked, and Billy heard the reticence and confusion in his voice. "Is that really you?" Darryl stood up and took a few steps forward, looking as though he was unsure of what he should do. Then he seemed to figure it out and hugged the other man. "My God." The smile on Darryl's face put one on Billy's as well. "How did you find me?" Darryl released the hug and stood there, looking awkward.

"I didn't." Connor looked at Billy. "He did."

"How?" Darryl's gaze alternated between the two of them as though he wasn't sure where to look first.

"He contacted me through my Facebook page." Connor looked around the restaurant as though he was taking everything in.

"Please, sit down, can we bring you anything? A soda? Beer?"

"No thanks, I'm fine." Connor sat in the booth, and Darryl slid in across from him. Billy wasn't sure if he should stay or not. He really wanted to hear what had happened, but he didn't want to intrude. Darryl made up his mind for him when he took Billy's hand and tugged him toward the booth. Then the three of them stared at each other, none of them knowing what to say. Billy's leg began to bounce as he wondered if this had been a good idea. God, what if Darryl was angry with him?

"What happened to you?" Both Darryl and Connor said at nearly the same time, and Billy could feel some of the tension slip away.

"Please." Darryl indicated that Connor should continue.

"After we were caught, my dad convinced himself that everything was all your fault. He told me his version of what you did and the 'therapy' program your folks were putting you in."

Billy looked to Darryl, who didn't say anything, but nodded slowly, and Billy could see the guilt and conflict on his lover's face. Billy hated that it was there, but he truly hoped that talking to Connor might help Darryl let go of some of those emotions. Darryl had told him that it was behind him, but Billy was smart enough to know that something like this didn't just disappear. Guilt was a powerful thing, and misplaced guilt could eat you alive if you let it.

"Dad began almost immediately making plans for us to move," Connor continued. "And he told me if I ever saw you again, he'd put me away." Connor swallowed, and Billy got up, stepping to the coffee station near the booth. "I was so scared, I didn't know what to do. I wanted to see you more than anything, but"—Connor lowered his eyes to the table—"I was scared shitless."

"Connor," Billy heard Darryl's voice begin as he poured three cups of coffee, "of course you were scared. Hell, I was scared of your dad too." Billy set the cups on the table. Sitting back down, he took Darryl's hand, wishing at the same time that there could be a way to comfort Connor as well.

Billy watched as Connor sipped from his cup. The man was handsome, not as handsome as his Darryl, but still nice-looking, with expressive eyes and short, dark hair. Billy scooted a little closer to Darryl as he listened.

"After we moved, I tried to find you a few times, but my dad kept such a close eye on me, I couldn't do much. When I went to college, I finally got to taste a little bit of freedom and ended up moving to the west coast." Connor smiled brightly, and Billy thought he caught a glimpse of what Connor must have been like when Darryl had known him. "It took a few years, but I told my dad where he could stick all his stupid religious crap. That was the last time we spoke."

The table got quiet, with only the occasional sip of coffee breaking the stillness. Unable to take it anymore, Billy nudged his lover in the side, but Darryl just looked down at the table. Billy hadn't seen that look since the night Darryl had first told him about

Connor and all the stuff those "doctors" had put him through. "Then I didn't ruin your life?"

"God, no." Connor set down his coffee. "I always thought I'd ruined yours. After all, you were the one who ended up in that place. If it was anything like what my dad threatened me with, it must have been sheer hell. I always thought you had to have blamed me for it."

Darryl shook his head. "No. It wasn't your fault. It was mine. I was older, and I was the one responsible."

"You sound just like my dad did. There was no fault or blame. We loved each other and did what kids do. I wouldn't have changed that part for anything." When Connor reached over the table to stroke Darryl's cheek, Billy had to stop himself from slapping the man's hand away. "You were my first love, and for that I'll always remember you."

"But your family," Darryl replied softly, just above a whisper. "I cost you so much."

"I think we both paid way too high a price just for falling in love." Connor's mug thunked as he set it on the table. "And as for my family, his name's Jerry, and he's waiting for me at home. He's all the family I need. But just so you know, my dad died a few years ago—one less small-minded bigot in the world. I talk to my mother occasionally, and she's slowly coming to terms with things. Maybe we'll have a relationship again, and maybe we won't."

They talked a little while longer. Darryl told Connor about his family and the twins. He even dragged out their pictures and some of their drawings. After about an hour, Connor pushed back his mug and stood up to leave. "It looks to me as though you've found someone to make you happy too." Billy felt Connor's gaze. "We were kids, Darryl, and we did what kids do. You have nothing to feel guilty or ashamed about. Whatever those doctors told you were lies; all of it was lies."

Billy stood up, and Connor shook his hand as Darryl slid out of the booth behind him. Saying farewell, Connor gave Darryl a hug and walked toward the door. He turned and waved through the window before disappearing down the sidewalk.

Billy felt arms around his waist, and then he was engulfed in a warm hug.

"You're not mad, are you?" Billy asked tentatively.

"How could I be?"

Billy felt himself being turned around and then kissed hard. "I wasn't sure if you'd want me interfering." Billy felt Darryl's lips slip away, and then he was taken by the hand and almost dragged through the kitchen door and into the office, the door slamming shut behind them. With an *ooof,* Billy found himself pressed against the wall, being kissed within an inch of his life. Billy put his arms around Darryl's neck and held on as Darryl's body pressed against his. Any more questions he might have had flew from his head as Darryl's tongue pressed for entrance. "Darryl," Billy gasped softly as he tried to get purchase against his lover's body. "We can't do this here." But damn, he wanted to get naked and climb the man, he was so turned on. Billy felt Darryl step back, those lips gentling the kiss.

"I know." Darryl looked into his eyes. "What you did was one of the nicest things anyone's ever done for me. How did you find him, anyway? You couldn't have known that much about him."

"I may not have known much, but your mother does. She told me his father and mother's names, as well as a bunch of information I was able to use to track him down. It really wasn't too hard once Kelly helped me with the computer stuff."

"Did everyone know about this but me?" Darryl sounded slightly annoyed.

Billy shook his head. "No one knew but me and maybe your mom, a little bit. The lucky part was that while Connor lives in San Francisco, he travels to the east coast on business and was in Philadelphia for a conference. He agreed to drive over to see you." Billy rested his head on Darryl's chest.

"So...." Darryl did his best to sound gruff, but Billy wasn't buying it, not with those hands stroking lightly along his back. "What else have you and my mom been talking about?"

Billy found himself laughing quietly. "All kinds of stuff. She's a real nice lady, and she says she can't wait to meet me when they come for a visit." Her easy acceptance had been so unexpected for Billy. "So you're not mad?"

Billy felt a rumble in Darryl's chest. "No, I'm not mad. Actually, I'm relieved." Billy tilted his head so he could see Darryl's eyes. "I've carried all that guilt around for so long, I never really realized it was there."

"I'm glad. I kinda figured it was something that maybe you both needed."

"I think you were right." Darryl squeezed him tight, just holding him silently. A not-so-subtle knock on the door told them it was time to go back to work. "We'll pick this up later," Darryl growled, and Billy nodded in agreement. They were definitely going to continue this.

"THAT was a mad house," Billy commented softly to Sebastian as they watched the final customers finish their coffee. "My legs feel a foot shorter."

"Yeah." Sebastian leaned against the bar, and Billy saw him looking over the dining room. "But we kicked it. The tables are reset, and the room's cleaned. Once they're done, we can get out of here." They kept their voices low so they wouldn't disturb the diners.

"Why don't you take off? I'll see to them and clean up their table for tomorrow. I was going to wait for Darryl anyway." Sebastian had helped him out so many times, it was the least he could do.

"You sure?" Sebastian was suddenly excited at the prospect of going home a little early.

"You bet, go on."

Sebastian got his jacket and disappeared out the back. The customers finished their coffee and paid the bill, leaving a nice tip that Billy put into Sebastian's jar. "'Night." He waved as they left and then locked the door, breathing a huge sigh of relief. Cleaning the table, Billy put the bus tray with the dirty dishes aside and stripped the table linens, putting on the clean ones he'd set aside and setting the table before picking up the tray and carrying it to the dish room. "Hey, guys, this is the last of it." He set the tray down, and the boys began putting them through the dishwasher.

"When you're done, clock out and go home."

"Trying to get out of here, Billy?" One of the washers retorted as he opened the dishwasher, steam billowing out.

"Same as you," Billy teased, and they laughed in return, getting back to work as he left the room, walking toward the kitchen. Darryl was cleaning up for the night, the kitchen smelling slightly of bleach—clean and ready for the morning. "Sebastian is gone, and so are the rest of the servers and bussers. The dish room is finishing up."

"I'm ready here, so as soon as they're done, we can go." Darryl stepped closer, and it didn't matter how tired Billy was, his body was instantly ready to go. Then he was being held, and his excitement kicked up yet another notch. Darryl's lips slid along his neck. "If I live to be a hundred, I'll never stop loving you."

"We're ready," one of the dish washers said from behind him, and Billy heard the soft snickers, like he and Darryl had been caught doing something naughty.

Billy didn't move away. "Thanks, guys." It felt too good right where he was at the moment.

"We should go too. There's a big, soft bed waiting for us." Darryl began walking them toward the back door, with Billy practically hanging off him. He didn't seem to mind, and Billy had no intention of breaking contact with his lover unless he had to. Finally letting go, Billy stepped back. "Have you got everything?"

Making a quick detour to the office, Billy grabbed the envelope the twins had sent them. "I'm ready." Billy waited while Darryl turned off the lights, watching as the restaurant went dark. Stepping out into the summer night, Billy waited while Darryl locked the door. Darryl took his hand, and they walked to the car together for the short drive home.

In the house, Billy headed upstairs with Darryl right behind him. "You want a shower?" Darryl asked as they reached their bedroom.

"No, not right now," Billy whispered as he wound his arms around his lover's neck, bringing their lips together. "I believe we have some unfinished business from earlier." Billy didn't wait for a response. He'd been half hard for hours, the memory of their earlier kisses simmering all evening. He felt Darryl's hands on his back and then cupping his butt. Lifting his legs, he wound them around Darryl's waist and held on tight as he feasted on his lover's mouth. Billy's lips tugged and pulled on his lover's, their tongues dancing around and along each other.

Darryl carried him to the bed, but before Darryl could lower him to the mattress, Billy stood back up and maneuvered his lover back onto the mattress. "Tonight you're mine," Billy said huskily, and Darryl's eyes went wide momentarily. Billy kissed him again, tugging lightly on his lower lip to distract him. "You always show me how much you love me and care for me. Tonight it's your turn." Billy's fingers opened the buttons of his lover's shirt, parting the fabric, his lips and tongue following the trail of exposed skin. The taste of his lover's skin burst on his tongue, a unique blend of sweat, salt, masculinity, and spices that seemed to permeate him.

Kneeling on the bed, Billy ran his tongue over a tawny nipple, his lover whimpering softly as his tongue and lips worked the hard little buds. Those whimpers turned to outright groans when Billy slid his hand down Darryl's stomach and into his pants, fingers sliding along the thick length. Billy felt Darryl's hips thrust slightly, and he pulled his hand away before opening the belt buckle and parting the flaps of Darryl's pants. Thrusting the front of his lover's briefs out of the way, Billy freed Darryl's length, and he stroked his lover with what he knew had to be agonizing slowness as he took Darryl's lips in a possessive kiss.

"Billy." Darryl actually whined as he began thrusting through Billy's fingers.

Tightening his grip, Billy held his hand still, letting Darryl take what he needed. The man looked completely decadent: shirt hanging open, chest and stomach shining with sweat, pants open, his cock sliding through Billy's fingers, a look of expectant bliss on his face. "Take what you want," Billy coached softly, and Darryl's thrusting picked speed and urgency, his breath and the small cries that accompanied it coming hard and faster.

Darryl's length throbbed in his hand. "Billy!" Darryl's shout filled the room as he came in explosive torrents, stomach clenching, lungs gasping for breath.

Billy brought his lips to Darryl's, kissing him hard. He felt Darryl's fingers slide under his shirt, and Billy broke the kiss long enough to pull the shirt over his head. Darryl pulled him close, warm hands rubbing along his back, lips tasting, kissing, loving. "I want to make love to you," Billy whispered softly. Darryl had always balked before, never giving that last part of himself. Billy knew why, but he hoped that things might be different now that Darryl could let go of his guilt. "Want to show you what you give to me." Billy ran his hand over Darryl's chest, but Darryl said nothing, his eyes widening, watching. "Let me love you?" Billy coaxed gently. "You're worthy of being loved, Darryl. Connor loved you, and I love you. Let me show you just how much."

"Yes." Darryl's answer was barely above a whisper, sounding like an almost-silent plea.

Billy kissed his lover softly, their lips re-exploring familiar territory made wonderfully new as Darryl shed his shirt. Breaking the kiss, Billy pulled off Darryl's pants before opening his own and dropping them to the floor. Climbing back on the bed, he prowled toward his lover, and Darryl chuckled softly, that happy sound zinging through Billy like a shot of electricity. He wanted to make Darryl happy. With Billy's guidance, Darryl rolled onto his stomach, and Billy climbed the bigger man's body like it was a mountain of muscle.

Settling between Darryl's legs, Billy sucked and kissed the inside of those beefy thighs as Darryl's legs parted on their own. Moving closer, Billy kneaded the firm cheeks, kissing the hard flesh before spreading Darryl's cheeks. Darryl was unusually quiet. Running his tongue along the crack, Billy zeroed in on his lover's small pink opening, and the silence ended in a hoarse cry of surprised delight. "Billy, God." Darryl thrust back, mashing Billy's face to Darryl's butt, driving his tongue into the flesh.

Grabbing Darryl's legs for purchase, Billy thrust deep into his lover's opening, his lover's deep musk bursting on his tongue. Darryl's cries turned to soft whimpers, and Billy felt the muscles loosen around him. Billy loved it when Darryl did this for him, and while he didn't have a great deal of experience taking charge, he knew how he liked Darryl to love him, and he reciprocated with gusto. "You like that?"

"Uh-huh," Darryl moaned softly from the head of the bed, body rocking slightly with what Billy knew was intense pleasure. There was no doubt that Darryl was completely turned on. His lover's back was arched, and Billy could feel small movements as Darryl ground into the sheets.

"Are you ready for me, love?"

"God, yes," Darryl gasped. "How do you want me?"

Billy crawled up Darryl's back until he was lying on top of him, skin to skin, sucking lightly on Darryl's ear. "I want to see you, get lost in those eyes of yours."

Billy straddled his lover, getting himself ready while Darryl shifted on the bed. Darryl brought his knees to his chest and Billy moved close, pressing himself to the opening.

Nothing happened at first. Then, slowly, Billy felt Darryl's body open for him, and he was surrounded by hot, moist heat that made his head throb and his vision blur. "So full," Darryl muttered softly, and Billy stopped, just like Darryl had always done for him. Billy forced himself to wait until Darryl moved before pressing further. Those few seconds felt like the longest in his life. Billy's body threatened to draw him forward, driving him to join with his life-mate. Finally, Darryl touched his leg and Billy surged forward, burying himself deep in Darryl's warmth.

Already breathing like a marathoner, Billy waited, leaning forward to capture Darryl's lips. "Love you so much." The words felt inadequate to express everything he was feeling right now, but it was all his suddenly enfeebled brain would allow. Darryl's fingers carded through his hair, and he returned the kiss as Billy began to move.

Locking eyes with each other, they moved together, slowly at first, but then with increasing force and speed. Darryl's cries and moans mingled with Billy's, filling the room and the house with their shared, joyful love. Taking Darryl's reawakened thickness in his hand, Billy stroked to the rhythm of their love and Darryl's soft cries.

Feeling the familiar pressure building, Billy increased his grip, tugging harder, until he saw Darryl's eyes start to roll and felt Darryl's climax begin. Billy felt his legs shake as his own release crashed into him, and he buried himself, throbbing deep inside his lover's heat.

After his mind-blasting orgasm, it took Billy a few minutes for his eyes to refocus and his mind to start functioning again. But when it did, he saw his sated Darryl laid out in front of him, all glistening skin and heavy eyes. Darryl tugged him forward, and he slipped from his lover's body as strong arms enfolded him. Their lips came together in a languid kiss as fingers caressed cheeks, both nether and otherwise. Billy didn't want to move, not now, not ever.

"We should shower before we fall asleep and stick together," Darryl said, his eyes closing, mouth already yawning.

Billy pretended to mull over what Darryl had said. "Stuck to you. Hmmm, I think I could get used to that." He felt Darryl pull him in for another kiss.

"I hope so, because you're stuck with me for a very long time."

Stuck with him, stuck to him—didn't matter to Billy. He had his Darryl, and that was all that mattered. Getting out of bed, Billy grinned wickedly. "First one in the shower gets a blowjob!" Then he raced toward the bathroom, Darryl right behind him, their laughter filling the house.

EPILOGUE

"BILLY!" familiar high-pitched voices called out in tandem, and then he was inundated, getting hugs and listening to Davey and Donnie's welcome chatter about their trip. Thankfully he hadn't been carrying a tray of food, like the last time. He'd barely managed to set it down on the bar before the twins nearly toppled him over. Kneeling down, he returned their hugs, and then they were off into the kitchen to terrorize Darryl for a while.

Putting in the order he'd just taken, Billy looked over the dining room and saw people smile as they went back to their lunches. Hitting the submit button, the order placed, Billy looked up again and saw Marie and Charlie walk through the restaurant door, both of them beaming. They walked right up to him, Marie giving him a hug and then Charlie squeezing the air out of his lungs the way the big lug always did. "Would you like a table, or have you eaten already?"

"Are you kidding?" Charlie quipped. "We've been looking forward to Darryl's cooking for the last hundred miles."

Billy sat them at a large table, and the kitchen door opened. Darryl walked into the dining room with a boy hanging from each arm, both of them chattering away. "Sometimes I wonder if they even stop to breathe," Marie commented with an indulgent smile as she sat down, with Charlie holding her chair for her. "For the past week, they haven't stopped talking about all the things they were going to do while they were here."

Darryl approached the table, still carrying the now seven-year-old twins, the three of them laughing. The boys disengaged themselves and took their seats with just a minimum of chiding from their mother. "Can we go to the park after lunch?" The twins both looked up at Billy expectantly.

"Billy and Darryl have to work," Charlie informed the boys, receiving such looks of disappointment and dismay that you'd have thought the world was ending.

"Actually," Billy said, grinning, "as soon as Julio comes in, we're officially on vacation for the next week. So yes, this afternoon we'll go to the park, and tomorrow morning we leave." Billy could hardly believe it. He and Darryl were taking their first real vacation ever, and the twins were going along with them.

Sebastian brought crayons and paper to the table, chatting briefly before returning to his tables. The twins immediately went to work creating masterpieces. "So what do you want to eat?"

The boys didn't even raise their heads. "Chicken fingers." As if Billy didn't know.

Marie ordered the mussels, and Charlie had his favorite, the steak frites. Billy put in the orders and saw to the other tables before bringing drinks and a cone of fries for the boys. Then he made another round of his tables as the dining room began emptying as the lunch crowd thinned.

"I've got things under control," Sebastian said behind him. "Go join them and start your vacation."

"Thanks, Sebastian." The two of them had become close friends.

Billy took a seat at the table next to Davey. "So what's this big news you were hinting at?"

The kitchen door swung open, and Darryl walked into the dining room in his regular clothes. "What happened?" It was rare for anyone to see him out of uniform while he was in the restaurant.

"Julio kicked me out." Darryl feigned annoyance. "He said that for the next week, the kitchen was his, and that my big butt was crowding it." Darryl twisted around, looking for a second like he was trying to see his own ass.

Billy rolled his eyes. "Is that your way of asking if those pants make your butt look big?"

Marie and Charlie both started laughing. A second later, the twins joined in, not sure what was so funny but not wanting to be left out. Darryl looked miffed for a second and then began laughing as well, taking the seat across from Billy and next to Donnie. When the laughter died down, Billy looked expectantly at Charlie and Marie, prodding them to spill their news.

"Do you want to tell them?" Charlie asked Marie, but she shook her head.

"It's your news, you tell them." Her face was stern, and Billy felt worry start to rise.

"I got notification last week that I'm being promoted." Charlie grinned as Billy and Darryl offered him their congratulations. "With the promotion comes additional responsibilities and duties that aren't available at my current post."

Billy's fears seemed to be coming true. For the last two years, they'd made great efforts to allow him and Darryl to see the boys and had developed a close friendship in the process. He and Darryl had made numerous trips to Richmond, and the Hanovers had been up to Carlisle almost as many times. But those trips were always hard, and more distance between them would mean he'd rarely get to see his brothers. "Where are you being stationed?" Billy was afraid to ask, gulping water to quench his suddenly dry throat.

"The naval supply depot in Mechanicsburg."

Billy could hardly believe his ears. "You mean you're moving here?"

Charlie and Marie burst into huge smiles. "Yes. I have to report for duty in two weeks, and they'll move us here as soon as we find a house."

"If you need some help, I have a great real estate agent. I used him when I bought my house," Darryl offered, and he received a quick acceptance from both of them. "In fact, there's a house that's going to be for sale on the south side of town. We catered a party there at Christmas, and they told us they'd be moving this summer. The place is beautiful, with plenty of room, and it even has a pool in the backyard."

"Shouldn't we get an agent first?" Marie asked, excitement in her voice.

Darryl shook his head. "In this town, the good houses rarely hit the market. They're all sold through word of mouth. People have lived here all their lives and know everybody," Darryl explained as Sebastian brought plates.

"Julio said that your orders will be up in a few minutes," Sebastian said to Darryl and Billy before filling glasses and moving away.

Billy waited a few minutes and then headed into the kitchen. It seemed strange for Julio to be at Darryl's station, but he was a good chef and deserved the opportunity to show his stuff. Darryl hadn't said anything to anyone except Billy, but Darryl was hoping to open a second restaurant with Julio as the chef. This vacation was his trial run.

"You're all set." Julio placed the plates on the counter.

Billy took the plates. "Thanks. I think that's about the end of lunch." Julio nodded his acceptance and kept working.

"Say, Billy," Kelly called from behind Julio. "You and Darryl have a great time, and don't worry about a thing, I'll keep him in line." She swatted the chef with a towel before returning to her work.

Billy carried his and Darryl's plates to the dining room. Donnie had moved to his seat, he and Davey drawing together. Billy set down the plates and sat next to Darryl.

"So where are the four of you going? When we talked last week, you were still figuring out the schedule," Marie asked before popping a mussel into her mouth.

"We're going to Michigan to visit Darryl's family for a few days, and then on to Mackinac Island and the Upper Peninsula," Billy answered excitedly. He began eating as Darryl told all about their reservations at the Grand Hotel and about seeing waterfalls, picturesque rocks, and maybe bears. He was looking forward to their vacation. It didn't matter what they did or where they went—he was going to spend a week alone with his brothers and his partner. That was enough.

"What are you two drawing?" Darryl peered over the table to where the twins were diligently working.

Realizing they were being watched, they hid their drawing with their arms. "It's a surprise," Davey declared, and he went back to his work. The adults all smiled at one another and finished their lunches, continuing their conversation.

"It's done!" Donnie announced, standing on his chair, holding up the drawing as Davey explained, pointing to each figure.

"That's Mom and Dad, that's Billy and Darryl, and this is us." The words "Our Family" were printed unevenly along the top. "This is for you." Donnie jumped down from his chair, running around the table, handing the drawing to Billy, with Davey right behind him. Billy got hugs from both of them, as did Darryl, along with Mom and Dad for good measure.

"That's so true," Marie said softly. "The boys brought us all together."

"True," Billy agreed. "One of the most unconventional families you could imagine, but a family." Feeling emotional, Billy got up and began clearing the dishes, putting them on one of the nearby bus trays.

"You okay?" Darryl's hand touched him on the shoulder.

"Yeah." When he turned around, Darryl was standing very close. "I'm just fine." Billy looked back at the table. Charlie and Marie were talking softly; the twins were coloring. Then he let his gaze lift to Darryl. "I was just thinking how much I love you."

Darryl's hand squeezed slightly. "You say that now, but will you love me when I'm old and start turning gray?"

"Of course." Billy ran his fingers through the hair at Darryl's temple before kissing his cheek. "I got my taste of love, and it's you."

ANDREW GREY grew up in western Michigan with a father who loved to tell stories and a mother who loved to read them. Since then he has lived throughout the country and traveled throughout the world. He has a master's degree from the University of Wisconsin-Milwaukee and works in information systems for a large corporation. Andrew's hobbies include collecting antiques, gardening, and leaving his dirty dishes anywhere but in the sink (particularly when writing). He considers himself blessed with an accepting family, fantastic friends, and the world's most supportive and loving partner. Andrew currently lives in beautiful historic Carlisle, Pennsylvania.

Visit Andrew's web site at http://www.andrewgreybooks.com and blog at http://andrewgreybooks.livejournal.com/. E-mail him at andrewgrey@comcast.net.

Contemporary Romance by ANDREW GREY

http://www.dreamspinnerpress.com

Also by ANDREW GREY

http://www.dreamspinnerpress.com

Contemporary Fantasy by ANDREW GREY

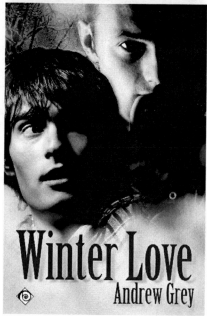